Brand-Changing Day

SHAWN MIHALIK

Asymmetrical Press
Missoula, Montana

Published by Asymmetrical Press
Missoula, Montana
www.asymmetrical.co

Library of Congress Cataloging-In-Publication Data
Brand-changing day / Shawn Mihalik — 2nd ed.
ISBN: 978-1-938793-24-0
eISBN: 978-1-938793-26-4
WC: 54,668
1. Restaurants. 2. Corporations. 3. Youngstown. 4. Death. 5. Black bears.

Cover design by Colin Wright
Formatted in beautiful Montana, U.S.A.

Author info:
Website: asymmetrical.co/shawn
Email: shawn@asymmetrical.co
Twitter: @shawnmihalik

ASYM METR ICAL

for Leslie

I really don't like going out. I don't like restaurants because I don't like the idea of someone, a waitress, being responsible for my evening. I like seconds, and more, and lots of conversation, and I've always hated the idea that in a restaurant an evening just ends. I find that incredibly depressing.
—AMY SEDARIS

Goodbye, Ruby Tuesday.
—KEITH RICHARDS

Brand-Changing Day

ONE

Four Months Pre Brand-Changing Day, 2012

During any given week, Earl's American Grill Restaurant Group, Inc. is embroiled in at least a half-dozen lawsuits, the natures of which often vary wildly from week to week and lawsuit to lawsuit, and so the company retains the services of a crackerjack legal team comprised of the partnerships of Gilbert & Worstman, Morell & Reinholdt, and Henderson, Henderson, Henderson & Gunn.

John Gilbert and Kenny Worstman, of Gilbert & Worstman, just last week settled out of court the case of a young woman who was suing The Grill after allegedly (and it had actually happened) eating a bowl of potato chowder, featured on the menu as "Cheesy Southern Potato Bisque," which contained in its thick soupy midst a broken metal fork tine. The tine had, allegedly (truthfully), become lodged in the young lady's—a Miss Gwen Day from New Haven, Connecticut—throat, and when her dining partner had attempted a sort of amateur Heimlich maneuver, the tine had dislodged as expected but had then torn a significant portion of Miss Day's esophageal lining, and Miss Day, who would eventually make a full recovery, had been unable to eat without a feeding tube for nearly a full month, and even after that she'd been allowed no solid food for weeks. Gilbert and Worstman, as was their prerogative, helped Miss

Day understand that, since her dining partner had been unqualified to perform the Heimlich maneuver or any other medical procedure at the time of the incident, a judge would likely see the damage to her esophagus as the companion's fault. And of course Earl's American Grill Restaurant Group, Inc. would be happy to take the matter to court, if that's what Miss Day really wanted, but they would hate to see Miss Day take on extensive legal expenses in a case she had little chance of winning. They weren't heartless, though, they told her, and they would be happy to write Miss Day a check for $20,000 right here and now if she would be willing to save herself the trouble and let the matter drop. And Miss Day, without speaking to her own attorney because she didn't yet have one, accepted the offer and used the money to buy a new car or a boat or something.

Beginning in the spring of 2003, shortly after the company's first major rebranding, the massive team at Henderson, Henderson, Henderson & Gunn, who specialize in trademark and copyright law, in their job for Earl's American Grill and Restaurant Group, Inc., had officiated a record 1,300 lawsuits in the span of six months, each one initiated by the company and each one settled in the company's favor.

At the same time that Earl Bradford, Jr., decided to truncate his restaurant's name, there existed in the United States over 20,000 restaurants, some of these large or small chains but most of them single-location independently owned and operated establishments, named either "The Grill," "The Grille," or otherwise utilizing the words "grill" or "grille" in their branding. E. E. Bradford, in an attempt to capitalize on trademarks he and his late brother had registered over twenty years before, took the fight first to the smaller mom-and-pop restaurants. At Bradford's lawyer's behest, many of these companies simply changed or shortened their names, removing the offending word, and that was the end of it, while others, those companies whose owners were idealistic or even just overly nostalgic, fought until the legal costs became too large a burden on their business accounts or personal pocketbooks, and most of the smaller restaurants that had lawsuits brought against them by The Grill buckled under the financial and legal pressure, closing their doors permanently within six months of said lawsuits' filings. And if he'd actually been bothered to check in with his lawyers from time to time, Earl E. Bradford might have taken pity on some of these small businesses' owners—owners who might have reminded him so much of himself and his brother way back when—and his heart might have softened toward them a little, and he might have dropped the suits and infringement cases. But then again, realistically, that's probably not what would have happened, and as it was, once the idea to stake his trademark claim had been communicated to the lawyers who would do the staking, Earl Bradford's interest in the matter waned completely and he let the attorneys do their jobs while he moved on to other things. And so between 2003 and the present, Earl's American Grill Restaurant Group, Inc. had catalyzed the failure of roughly 15,000 independent businesses, and most weeks it helped facilitate the demise of at least one or two more, although they had yet to tackle the big chains, like, for example, Applebee's International Inc., which operates Applebee's Neighborhood Grill and Bar.

In recent weeks, The Grill's crackerjack legal team had taken it upon themselves—that is, assigned a group of unpaid law-student interns with hopes of possibly working for the legal team of Earl's American Grill Restaurant Group, Inc. after the internship was over—to compile a plan for bringing to suit all

American restaurant chains with 200 stores or less who used as their brand colors midnight black, Alizarin Crimson, or any combination thereof, which colors/combinations the crackerjack legal team had been attempting to patent since 2003 (and even though these patent requests had been repeatedly denied on the grounds that an "individual or legal entity, corporate or otherwise, cannot claim ownership of any one specific color," the lawyers comprising the crackerjack legal team were confident that they would, eventually and soon, come to some sort of head with the U.S. Patent Office in which one of them, i.e. the patent office or the legal team, would give up—and it certainly wasn't going to be the legal team). After the group of hopeful interns had compiled a satisfactory plan, for no pay and while making immeasurable amounts of very dark, very burnt coffee, the crackerjack legal team, represented in this instance by Garrison (Gary) Gunn, had brought the plan before Earl Bradford Jr. and his board of directors.

Interest in the plan was mixed: Half of the eight-person board of directors—including Rebecca Loor, Ryan Penstock, James J. Ornithalt, and Eliot Flagswagger—thought the plan was a fantastic way to assert a measure of corporate power, but the other half—namely, Peter Glenlow, Stephen L. Hubbard, Gloria Reinwell, and Earl Bradford, Jr., himself—wondered aloud if maybe Earl's American Grill Restaurant Group, Inc. was beginning to spread itself too thin, legally.

"Of course not," argued 71-year-old Ornithalt, stroking his tobacco-stained white handlebar mustache with his left hand and fiddling with his brown corduroy tie with his right, speaking in a gruffly shrill smoker's voice. "Why, just look at the success our teams've had so far. We've never lost a case, I don't believe. Have we?"

Ornithalt looked at Gunn with uncertainty, and Gunn shook his head. They'd never lost a case, and certainly Gunn's team had never lost a patent or trademark suit.

"See," Ornithalt grunted.

Ultimately, though, the matter didn't even come to a vote, because Earl E. Bradford, Jr., announced that he would like to, with the board's approval, of course, engage the company in another structured rebranding, the details of which he'd been working on for some time.

The boardroom grew quiet, and Loor leaned forward, speaking for the lot of them. "Go on." Her accent was British. She was from Oregon.

And so Bradford launched into a detailed account of his plan, complete with printed spreadsheets and demonstrative charts, his voice his particular brand of Texan drawl. The experimental dishes the company had recently been testing in various North American stores and also the dessert menu they'd rolled out in the North East U.S. a few months ago were so far very well received by customers, and so now was the time to make them permanent fixtures, introduce a new menu company-wide, and while they were at it, why not do a wider rebranding. No name changes this time, of course, but new uniforms, new procedures, time to get rid of the shades of red from the company's logo altogether and change the black to a brighter, less midnight sort of black. And of course there was a good deal more to it, which they could discuss soon, but here was the clincher: they could get the ball in motion quickly, roll out the changes in just a few months, and then, maybe six months after that, announce the company's IPO.

This last point was the linchpin of Bradford's plan. Several of the board members had wanted to take the company public for some time now. Others had been indifferent, happy with the money they were currently making, content to also manage the stakes they held in other various private companies. Earl E. Bradford had been adamantly against it. So when he announced his plan and his acquiescence to—or rather, more appropriately, his *avidity toward*—the idea of a public stock offering, the rest of the board applauded, Ornithalt and Hubbard enthusiastically so.

Brand-Changing Day, 2012

The curtains, hand-made by his wife's mother and given to them as an anniversary present after seven years of marriage, diffused, but only slightly (for the curtains, while hand-made, were poorly made and thus the various stitchings had come loose long ago and holes had grown along the seams) the light of the moon, which shone across the room and over Geoff McCree's looks-older-than-it-really-is face. Geoff had seen the curtains hanging in his wife's mother's kitchen—the kitchen was not his wife's father's, oh no; the kitchen, it seemed, according at least to Maynard James, his wife's father, belonged to the woman, and the rest of the house to the man (except for the corner of the den nearest the door, which belonged to the dog, in this case a dark-brown retriever named Walden)—years before they had ever married, and while he'd observed once to his wife that the curtains weren't made specifically for them and that presenting them as such was a generally heartless and dishonest gesture—that is, a lie—his wife urged him to feel grateful, so he tried. Tonight he tried to sleep, turning left and turning right, burying his face in his pillow and then unburying it. He tried pulling the coffee-colored comforter, a larger-than-necessary and far too warm adornment, over his head, attempting to shield his eyelids from the moonlight that snuck through the poorly stitched seams in the curtains over the window, the moonlight refusing to release the grasp it held on the slumber Geoff McCree desired, but he found the comforter firmly anchored to the bed by his wife's sleeping body. Geoff, despite having worked more than eighteen hours consecutively of the previous twenty-four, did not *crave* sleep so much as he just kind of wanted it. He tried to envy his wife for sleeping so well and so easily, but instead he just sort of wished he could do the same as her. Just sort of.

She—Geoff's wife—shifted in the bed, rolling over onto her right side so that her serene face now faced Geoff's blank one. Geoff recalled, in the part of his mind reserved for such thoughts as this one, that his wife preferred sleeping on her stomach, which she hadn't been able to do in several months both because pregnant women aren't supposed to do such things and because, even if the doctor hadn't told her doing so could harm the fetus, sleeping on a stomach that large and round and firm would, Geoff imagined, cause high levels of discomfort, what with the way the back would arch and both the shoulders and hips would point downward, putting pressure on the trachea (Geoff didn't actually know the word trachea; he thought of it, on the rare occasions he thought of it, as the "breathing tube") and making it difficult but not impossible to breathe. Even standing with a belly as large as his wife's was uncomfortable, so he'd been told. The moon continued to shine through the pathetic curtains, and Geoff considered that he kind of wanted to have sex with his wife because he hadn't since the night she'd gotten herself pregnant with his child eight months ago, but instead he just stared at the curtains.

* * *

Only hours later, Geoff McCree, aged 42 years and counting, stared noncommittally down at the paunch that one might be inclined to call his midsection. The water—as hot as he could handle on this (a Tuesday) morning, which was to say, not very —poured down from somewhere above his head, its source a garishly large flat chrome shower head, which he'd purchased for nearly three hundred dollars at his wife's insistence, and which, despite its massive bigness (Geoff knew there were better words than "bigness" but could think of none), actually produced a stream of frustratingly little pressure. It turned out, in fact, that the shower head—a *Wettech Superspray 2500*—wasn't designed to emit a *superspray*, but rather the purpose of the large apparatus was to conserve water. Geoff cared little about conserving water. (Geoff, after purchasing the *Wettech* and discovering its disappointing spray, had complained about it one day, as one might, to one of his employees, Scott, who then ranted about the fact that most of the world was annoyingly unaware that water, while not necessarily a renewable resource, cannot be wasted: the water cycle, as Scott exclaimed, works in such a way that any water one may use for any task—washing a car, cooking, drinking, etc. and whatever—even if such use is excessive, will be either evaporated into the atmosphere or released into the ground, ocean, lake, or other body, and eventually and naturally cleaned and used again. Geoff did not understand the rant, but he thought of it, and by proxy, Scott, now whenever he showered.) He stared down at the paunch of his belly. It had grown in the last few months, he was aware, similar to his wife's, except that where his wife's weight gain was a symptom of new life growing inside her, Geoff's was a symptom of a failure to integrate any real dietary principles into his daily routine. (Again, Geoff neither knew the meaning of the word integrate—

although he'd heard it before, he would never have thought to use it in a sentence himself—nor had more than a cursory [another word he would not have used] awareness of his own principles, dietary or otherwise.)

Geoff reached for the bar of Dove soap that sat in the little porcelain soap dish coated with a few of his own body hairs and began to lather the paunch. He lathered his arms, his legs, his genitals, the portions of his back that he could reach without a loofa, which he didn't own; and then, because he didn't feel like reaching for the bottle of Alberto VO8 shampoo, strawberry scented, that sat on the ledge of the bathtub, he massaged the Dove soap into his scalp as well.

Geoff stayed like that, covered from head to toe in rich, foamy, flesh-cracking lather, for several minutes, his eyes closed and his mouth hanging slightly open so the semi-hot water from the *Wettech* washed some of the soap from his hair onto his tongue. He hardly noticed the bitter flavor. He nearly fell asleep like that but didn't. He rinsed the lather from his body, turning the water temperature up but then deciding it was too hot and turning it back down again.

The clock on the stand by the bed said 7:02, and Geoff's wife was still asleep, having wrapped the comforter tightly around her entire body, exposing the sheet on the half of the bed where Geoff had been sleeping to the stale morning air. Geoff finished drying and tossed his towel onto the high-backed leather chair in the corner of the bedroom where his wife would find it later that morning. He knew she might have something to say to him when he returned home about leaving his laundry lying around, but he also knew she would take the towel into the basement and add it to the rest of the washing anyway.

He walked quietly over to the large oak dresser he and his wife shared and opened one of the drawers—the leftmost one on the top—and pulled out a white T-shirt and opened another drawer—the leftmost one in the middle—and pulled out a pair of blue jeans which were faded and worn and only slightly baggy. He put on both the jeans and the shirt and a pair of black socks and a pair of black non-slip shoes, the kind required of nearly all those who worked in restaurants, and tiptoed out of the bedroom and into the hallway and then into the living room. He considered, briefly, stepping into the kitchen and making a few pieces of toast, but decided otherwise. He would stop instead again at the Dunkin' Donuts over on Route 46 and pick up one of those, whatayacallthem, croissants with the processed cheese and the sausage patty and the egg-beater-type-things and the grease that dripped precariously down your chin and onto your pants or shirt if you weren't very careful about keeping the paper wrapping still on the sandwich as you ate.

Geoff stopped near the door that led to the garage and pulled out an ugly blue and yellow jogging jacket, size L, emblazoned with the logo of his favorite American football (Geoff was unaware of the existence of other kinds of football) team and put it on. It wasn't supposed to be particularly cool outside, but he had to do pulls this morning, and it could get rather cold in the walk-in after more than a few minutes. Geoff opened the door to the garage and walked through. He got in the car, started the ignition and, reaching up for the device connected to the sun visor, activated the large garage door, allowing bright early morning light—the sun had just nearly finished rising—to pour into the garage against the rearview mirror and into Geoff's green eyes, forcing him to blink repeatedly and settle on a lengthy squint before adjusting to the luminance. He started to back out into the driveway, but stopped. He remembered forgetting something.

Geoff got out of the car after placing it in park, leaving the keys in the ignition, and ran back into the house. He returned moments later with his black iPhone, which he plugged into the sedan's AUX jack—only recently a standard in cars and trucks, etc.—and activated his favorite mobile application, one of the incredibly dull, gratuitous digital affairs dedicated solely to sports and sports-related talk radio and the streaming of such over 3- and-4G data networks.

Brand-Changing Day, 2012

The man walked into the room, his gait blithe yet stiff at the same time, carrying an important-looking leather briefcase, which he placed on the floor near the lectern with a thud like that an elephant might make were its hind legs to suddenly just altogether disappear from beneath its massive body. He cleared his throat and turned around to face the chalkboard, which was the same green color as the ocean, and which was clean and clearly rarely used. The man seemed to be searching for a stick of chalk with which to write but was having trouble finding one until he turned back toward the lectern. He half nodded—brought his head back so that his forehead pointed at the high lecture hall ceiling for a moment before bringing it back to the default head position—and raised his eyebrows like he should have known the chalk would be there on the lectern and probably certainly should have looked there first. He turned back toward the board, touched the chalk to it, and started writing and speaking at the same time. "Good morning, ladies and gentleman. I am Dean"—strong emphasis on the word *dean* —"Charles Bligh, and I'll be teaching this class, Introduction to Communication, this semester."

Lori sat three rows back from the lectern, a notebook open on the table in front of her and in which she was doodling in a dark lavender ink. Her pen had one of those feathers sticking out the end. She drew a vertical line, applying heavy pressure so the purple ink soaked into the paper, giving the line a soft, blurry thickness.

Dean Charles Bligh was wearing a brown suit that, while plain, flattered his broad shoulders and did a decent job of hiding the loose spare tire around his midsection. His shirt was that shade of blue that every man should own at least one shirt of, and his tie, which was polyester and knotted in a full-windsor, was a pale yellow that complimented the blue and the brown. His head was round and his hair grey and thin and slicked back with almost too much product, and he wore those glasses with thick frames that are rounded at the bottom and straight at the top. He had thick eyebrows whose hairs looked like they might have recently had a balloon rubbed up against them.

Lori didn't notice these details. In fact, she hadn't looked at Dean Bligh once since he'd entered the lecture hall. She finished the two-inch vertical line, which had curved just slightly with the movement of her hand and, never raising her pen from the paper, moved the pen to the right about a quarter-inch and then began another vertical line from there, this time drawing upward.

"I don't normally teach this class. In fact I don't normally teach at all because I'm a *dean*"—there was the emphasis again, which Lori heard even though she wasn't looking—"but the professor who was scheduled to teach it will unfortunately be out the rest of the semester. Due to family problems, I think."

Lori stopped after two inches, then drew to the right again a quarter-inch, and then up a quarter-inch, left a quarter-inch, up a quarter-inch.

"But that's okay, though, because I'm excited to be teaching this class. Communication is actually one of my favorite subjects —I'm the Dean of English, after all—and I've got a fascinating curriculum prepared. You could say I'm most passionate about communication. It is, after all, the basis for our, well, communication. But the curriculum. We're going to talk a great deal about Carl Jung and the hierarchy of needs, that is, Maslow's hierarchy, not Jung's. Jung wrote about the archetypes, not the hierarchy . . . Anyway, the hierarchy, Maslow's, includes physiological needs, like sex and food, the need for self-actualization, love and belonging . . ."

What any of that would have to do with basic communication related to her major of education with a focus on kindergarten through fourth grade, Lori wasn't sure. She moved the pen to the left a quarter-inch, down a quarter-inch, left a quarter-inch, down a quarter-inch, right a quarter-inch, connecting the pen with the first line she'd drawn.

Dean Bligh coughed. He'd written his name on the chalkboard along with the first syllable of the word hierarchy, and he'd managed to conjure quite a bit of chalk dust.

Lori colored in her drawing so that now it was a solid, bluish-purple cross. Underneath it she wrote, "I love him." And then she crossed out "him" and wrote it again, capitalizing the H so that it said, "Him." And then she just scribbled over the whole thing—the cross and the words—violently before tearing the sheet of paper out of the notebook so she could take notes on the next sheet and pay attention.

The dean was back at writing on the board again, finishing *hierarchy*, and he was talking again too, but he was facing the board, and so his words were for the most part indecipherable academic mumblings, the perfect synecdoche of the entirety so far of Lori's college experience, of which she was starting her third semester.

"Hey," the red-haired girl in the seat to Lori's right whispered.

Lori turned to the girl who she'd only just met. They'd talked a bit before class, enjoying a superfluous conversation until the dean had walked in, almost fifteen minutes late; and if first impressions meant anything, Lori thought the girl was nice, but she couldn't remember her name. "What?" Lori whispered back.

"You said you worked at that restaurant, The Grill, right?"

"Yeah . . ."

"Have you heard about what's happening over there?"

"What do you mean? Right now? What's happening?"

"I don't know. Yeah. Something bad. Here, look, it's on Facebook and, like, the news."

One Month Pre Brand-Changing Day, 2012

Crack! Crack! Crack!

Many people seem to think—likely having had their expectations colored by American cinema and primetime television—that a gun when it goes off—that is to say, when someone picks it up, holds it in a grip that may or may not be quivering and anxious, may or may not be steady and vice-like—makes a sound like a cannon or a stick of dynamite, powerful and thunderous and deep. But this usually isn't true, at least not with the types of guns that most have the opportunity to fire—these guns tend to have a hollow, empty sound. They are, however, quite loud.

Take a gun like this one, for example: a .375 RugerTex Commercial Convex Contender, Premium Edition, released in 2010 to much acclaim from hobbyists and a reception more concordant with the word "meh" from rifle and pistol enthusiasts. This gun has an 18-inch barrel, made from a bored-out steel tube lined interiorly with a bronze/chrome composite, which by necessity is capable of withstanding the expanding force of something like 40,000 psi (pounds-per-square-inch) of combined gases as they push the bullet forward and out of the barrel toward the target. When this (the expelling of the gases) happens, the resulting sound is somewhere near 170 dB, assuming of course that the gun is equipped with a muzzle brake, which the .375 RugerTex Commercial Convex Contender, Premium Edition, is. Were it not, the sound would be far louder.

This was the gun Richard James Frederickson, who went by the more succinct R.J. Frederickson, had just now fired into the middle of a small clearing on the property of a friend of his in the wilderness of Hampshire County, West Virginia. He was wearing hearing protection—two small orange pieces of memory-foam which he'd inserted, one into each ear, earlier that morning—but the crack of the rifle was nevertheless loud. A long time ago, a very long time ago, R.J. might have— correction: *would* have—jumped at the sound and the recoil, may have even failed to hold his hands and arms and body steady enough as he pulled the trigger and smacked the rifle butt into his face just above the eyebrow requiring seven or eight stitches, but such things didn't happen to him now. He was thirty-two years old and had been shooting for twenty, just as long as he'd been working in the restaurant industry. Hence, every time he fired a rifle or a pistol or a shotgun, he had no problem remaining calm and steady; it was like a meditation for him. He was also very good at hitting his target.

But no one, not even the best hunters in the world, can kill their target every time, and R.J. cursed as his target today—a particularly large male black bear which he estimated at around 400 pounds—staggered off unsteadily but quickly into the woods. R.J. had obviously hit the creature, but it appeared the injury was less than serious, and he knew that finding the bear now and finishing it off would be more than difficult.

R.J. lowered the gun from the firing position and thumbed the safety switch to the left so he wouldn't accidentally fire the gun, which he tucked under his right arm as he reached into his front bottom-left pocket with his leather-gloved hand and pulled out a cigarette. From the same pocket he produced a gun-metal lighter. He fumbled awkwardly with the lighter and the cigarette for several seconds before pulling one glove off and tucking it also under his right arm with the rifle. He placed the cigarette between his lips and, his hand now uncovered and his fingers free to be dexterous, flicked the little wheel on the lighter, creating a flame and igniting the tip of the cigarette. He tucked the lighter back into his pocket, zipped the pocket, and grabbed the paper from his lips with his thumb and index finger. The cigarette was of no particular brand—that is to say, R.J. had paid no particular attention to the brand when purchasing the pack because cigarettes were all the same, right, just tobacco and nicotine and a few hundred other noxious chemicals and they would all kill you anyway, so why not just buy the ones that are cheapest, right?

The snow made a crunch-crunch noise beneath R.J.'s boots as he shuffled his feet. The winter had been warmer than usual, but this week had been something more akin to that which one expects, with temperatures in the high-twenties and low-thirties and snow that didn't melt as soon as it touched the ground. It all made it easier to spot the black bears, since they were black and all. The smoke from R.J.'s cheap cigarette lifted past his nose as he raised the paper back to his lips and took a drag. The snow crunch-crunched. R.J. inhaled deeply through his nose, trying to clear the snot out of his nasal cavities, successfully even, even though they began to fill again immediately thereafter. Crunch-crunch.

R.J. finished the cigarette and tossed it into the snow and, although he didn't actually hear it do so, he imagined that it sizzled as it made contact. He reached into his bottom-right pocket and fingered around inside until he'd opened a plastic zip-lock bag from which he pulled a strip of home-made jerky his buddy, who wasn't much of a hunter himself but who owned something like a thousand acres of land or something and was always happy to let R.J. hunt on it provided R.J. had the proper licenses in order and whatnot, had given R.J. that morning before he had headed out. He popped the jerky into his mouth and re-zipped the pocket and put his leather glove back on and shifted the gun so that it was no longer tucked uncomfortably under his arm. He checked the safety again—it was still on—and thumbed it back over to the right. He held the gun out in front of him with both hands, careful to keep the barrel pointed toward the ground diagonally so he could raise it quickly if need be but couldn't unintentionally shoot at a moving target otherwise. The jerky was smoky and tough and tasted of teriyaki and caramel. Combined with the lingering taste of the cigarette's tobacco, the jerky was revolting. R.J. twisted his neck to the right, cracking it, and moved off into the trees in the direction the injured black bear had gone.

Crunch-crunch.

Ten Months Pre Brand-Changing Day, 2012

"And so, then, Scott, tell me a little about yourself."

Twenty-two year old Scott Pelletier took a sip of the glass of ice water he'd been offered at the beginning of the interview. (Actually, he'd been offered, specifically, a soda, or as they had always called it here in Northeast Ohio, where Scott had lived his entire life since the time he was seven years old, save for a brief period of about a year that ended several months before, *pop*. But Scott didn't drink soda/pop, and hadn't in quite some time, because unlike most Americans he considered himself at least somewhat conscious of what substances—food, drink, medication and other drugs—he put into his body [which did not preclude him from getting drunk, on occasion], and he was aware, again unlike most Americans, that soft-beverages usually contained poisonous, obesity- and diabetes-inducing substances like high-fructose corn syrup, which is just a kind of highly processed sugar and like any sugar can spike insulin and blood pressure to dangerous levels, and the ingestion of which, if maintained for long periods of time—say, many months or years—can have disastrous health consequences, so he'd declined the soda, and when Geoff, the manager with whom he was interviewing, had pressed the issue of bringing him some sort of beverage, had simply asked for a glass of ice water instead, no straw, thank you. And also then it should be, and in fact is being, now, noted that Scott, when thinking thoughts about the ignorance of most Americans on matters of diet and health, thought them with an arrogance and piousness of which he had recently become grossly aware and which he was trying—struggling but trying—to curtail.) He wasn't sure how to answer the question, since it was such a vague and uninteresting one, and was silent for a moment before saying, "What, specifically, would you like to know?"

Geoff—his name was Geoff, he'd told Scott when Scott had spoken to him on the phone about Scott's application and they'd agreed to sit down for an interview on this afternoon, a Thursday, at two o'clock, which interview had started late, at a time closer to two-fifteen or two-twenty, because Geoff had been otherwise engaged with a particularly busy lunch shift or something—didn't shrug or move except to push Scott's application around on the table absently. "I dunno. Where are you from, I guess?"

Of course, the question had little relevance to, well, anything, except unless maybe Geoff had some sort of location bias toward potential hires, but Scott answered anyway. "Here," he said, "Ohio. Youngstown. Although I was born in San Diego and lived there until I was seven."

Geoff sort of maybe raised an eyebrow. "San Diego? You a Chargers fan?"

Scott shrugged. "Eh, a bit, maybe, but I'm not terribly into football. More of a hockey fan if anything, but not even that, really; I just don't care much for sports. But, anyway, I moved here when I was seven."

Geoff didn't really nod. "It says on your application that

your last job was at a Groovy Burger in Pittsburgh. How did you manage that?"

"What? To get a job at a Groovy Burger?"

"To work in Pittsburgh. Why did you work in Pittsburgh?"

"Oh." Scott nodded. "Because I lived there. For a while."

Geoff pushed the application around some more.

"So why'd you leave Pittsburgh then? Why'd you move back here?"

"Family emergency."

Geoff didn't ask for details, but for a moment Scott felt like making up some. "My sister—" he started to say, but of course he had no sister.

"Do you have any plans to leave again?"

Scott frowned. "Leave again?"

"Yeah." Geoff's voice, one might note, was deep and gruff and grunty in the way that a caveman's might have been. "Like, if I hire you, you don't have plans to leave Youngstown again or anything."

"I don't *think* so." Scott couldn't imagine a worse fate than staying in this city forever. He'd already tried to get away once, and he certainly planned on doing it again, albeit with longer term success.

"Alright. Well, look, I've already seen your application, so this interview is really just because. You've got plenty of experience it looks like, so let's go for it. Why don't you come back next Tuesday, say," Geoff leafed through the pages of the two-page application like he was looking for something, "how about nine o'clock?"

"Sure. Sounds good," Scott said, grinning in a way that made him look far more excited about the job than he should have been.

A young woman—a waitress—long blonde curly hair, thin, not short but not tall either, maybe Scott's age, appeared at the table, a twenty-dollar bill in her hand held out in front of her. "Geoff, sorry to interrupt," she said, "but I need change for a—"

"I'll be there in a minute," Geoff said. The girl frowned and walked away, and Geoff began to stand, picking up the two pieces of paper and sorting them and banging the edge of the two-page stack against the surface of the table in the way one does to make sure all the pages of a stack are even, flush with one another, so the stack is neat and tidy. Scott stood with him and held out his hand for a shake, but Geoff seemed more than necessarily preoccupied with the papers and either ignored or didn't notice the hand.

"Well, thank you . . ." Scott said. He was wearing dark jeans and a dark blue, button-down shirt.

"Thank *you*," Geoff said, looking up from the papers. And then he seemed to notice the hand because he reached out and shook it. "Hey, by the way, you need to be in uniform when you come in for orientation, so wear like a, like a black t-shirt and black pants, and you need to have a black belt, too, and black shoes, you know—you've worked in restaurants—the non-slip kind."

As Scott walked over to the door, he found the blonde waitress standing at the hostess station at the front of the restaurant. She smiled at him and he smiled back and she winked, and he would have winked back except he was never good at winking and didn't want to embarrass himself by trying, so he just kind of waved and walked out the door and into the sunlight.

* * *

Scott Pelletier was born in San Diego, California, to two young newly-weds. His mother, Lydia Pelletier, born Lydia McCormick, was out of high school only three months when she'd married. She'd been a brainy young lady, and she'd graduated early at sixteen with the intent of attending UCSD on a full government scholarship, majoring in business or law or politics, and working her way into the state senate and then, when she was good and ready, Washington and eventually the White House—maybe as speaker of the house or chief of staff or something like that, but not as president, because in 1988 nobody, or at least not Lydia McCormick, could honestly believe there could ever be a female president, no way, it just wasn't something that would happen. Fast-forward to 2012 and only four years earlier the country had come just *this close* to that very reality, and maybe if Lydia McCormick had stayed on the somewhat blurry-but-inarguably-aimed-at-least-in-some-general-direction path she'd imagined for herself, there might actually have been a woman president in the White House, and that woman might have been Lydia McCormick. Or at the very least Lydia McCormick might have been a California state senator. But as it happened, Lydia graduated high school early at sixteen and almost immediately thereafter met and slept with Gary Pelletier, who was eighteen and handsome and smart and charming and distinctly Mexican, everybody who met him thought, for someone with a name like Pelletier.

It was only two weeks into her first semester at UCSD that Lydia McCormick discovered she was pregnant, and since she'd lost her virginity to Gary, the child was most certainly his, and when she told him this he was overjoyed and promised her that she and the child would have his full support if that's what she wanted. Lydia's family encouraged abortion—immediately they told Lydia she was too young for a child and she had so much going for her and a child would ruin everything. She couldn't go to school and raise a child, they said, and if not abortion then at the very least adoption. But Lydia would have none of that. She had Gary, and the baby would have Gary, and they would be okay, they really would. She couldn't imagine giving up her child.

Scott knew this story, and for neither abandoning nor aborting him he was eternally grateful to his mother. Really.

And so Lydia's mother—a woman not without her own hardships, who'd raised Lydia on her own since her own husband had died of leukemia when Lydia was only ten—effectively disowned her daughter, but not before first appearing in court with Lydia and Gary when they applied for their marriage license, a sort of final show of support, required by California law for minors wishing to marry, before withdrawing support altogether.

Gary and Lydia were married for a year. Gary worked odd jobs here and there, mostly manual labor, paying for their rented one-bedroom apartment in Chula Vista while a pregnant Lydia continued with school, studying the prerequisites that would allow her to study law and politics, which she'd now firmly decided on as her major and minor, in her second year of college. She met regularly with the university's career counselors and, with her husband, a marriage counselor, both of which had actually been mandated by the judge who issued their marriage license as a condition of approval, a standard practice in the case of marriages in which one or both of the wedded is under the legal age of adulthood. The marriage counselor was nothing but encouraging, which wasn't surprising since Lydia and Gary were happy together and excited about the upcoming birth of their child. The career counselors, on the other hand, were incredulous, at the very least. A teenage girl, pregnant out of wedlock and then married at sixteen, who thought she had a chance at a career in politics? Ridiculous, they said. Come on Lydia, let's be realistic here. There's no way this is going to fly in the real world. And what if you did run for political office some day? What if? You think this isn't going to come out that you were pregnant at sixteen? Think about it, really. Really think about this. We don't mean to discourage, but the future you imagine for yourself just isn't possible for someone in your situation. And really, whose fault is that, anyway? *Yours*, Lydia, not ours.

But Lydia didn't care. She saw no negatives in her situation —she was smart; she had an early start on education; she had a loving, responsible husband; and she was going to be a mother soon, and a great mother, too. She studied hard, and as if to spite the counselors, she studied even harder than she might have otherwise. And during it all she went to the OBGYN for regular prenatal exams, and they were going to have a girl, the doctor told them. And Gary said they should name the baby Octavia— it was his grandmother's name, he said, and Lydia had never met his family, who he rarely mentioned—and Lydia convinced herself that she liked the name, so why not. And she even found the time to attend *Lamaze* classes, which were very trendy in the late eighties in Southern California, two nights a week, and Gary even went with her most of the time, except when he was on an evening construction job for work.

It was during her Psychology 102 final, her very last class of her second semester, in May of 1989, that seventeen-year-old Lydia went into labor. Her water broke right there in the lecture hall as she penned an essay about the effects of fostering cognitive dissonance in scholarly argument re destructive cults. She didn't complete the essay, but that hardly concerned her, and she finished the year with a 3.8 GPA and the self-assurance that she would continue the next semester on scholarship. Labor lasted eight hours—she was young, after all, and the doctor told her that he was surprised the labor hadn't lasted longer, a girl her age—and although Gary wasn't able to make it to the hospital until the last two hours, when he was there he was there, and he held Lydia's hand and smiled with her and made her laugh and talked her through the whole process, through the pain and the delivery, and at the end of the day, just before midnight, their son was born, and they named him Octavius Scott Pelletier.

The summer was one of recovery and bonding for Lydia and her new family. Lydia was a small young woman, and after the delivery she developed a not-inconsequential case of postpartum thyroiditis, and the related hormone imbalance caused her a great deal of fatigue and a bit of moodiness and even some hair loss, but she didn't mind. She spent the next three months at home with her son, changing diapers and nursing and loving him dearly, while her husband worked extra during those months so they would be able to afford for him to work less and take care of the baby when Lydia went back to school in the fall, and in the evening when he wasn't working, Gary was right there with them, taking care of and loving them both. The baby, who was born rather small at just six pounds five ounces, grew at an impressive rate during the summer, and by the end of August he weighed nearly fourteen pounds and smiled and cooed at everyone and everything and cried only when he was hungry, and he had a head full of thick, soft, curly dark-brown hair. As for Lydia, a nutritious diet and a prescribed regimen of selenium supplements took care of her hyperactive thyroid, and as the fall semester approached, she was both excited and nervous to return to school.

But then one afternoon, a week before the start of classes, Lydia received a call from UCSD's administration department. They needed more information, it seemed, in order to transfer Lydia's transcripts as she'd requested.

And just what do you mean, transfer them? Transfer them where?

Why, to the University of Chesterson, of course, as per Lydia's request. The problem was they couldn't find the address for Chesterson's registration department, so if Lydia could provide that information, that would be great, and they would have everything sorted out in short order.

Lydia didn't understand. University of Chesterson? Transcripts? Registration department?

Yes, well, registration department or administration, either address would do. They already had the address for the financial aid office, of course, just like she'd given them, and they'd squared everything away with regards to her scholarship and had sent the check already and everything, and so, like they'd already said, if they could just have the address for the registration office, Lydia should have no problems starting classes at Chesterson next week.

By the time Lydia Pelletier received this unexpected and befuddling phone call, Gary Pelletier was already well outside the state of California, heading east in a Chrysler LeBaron he'd stolen from a Vons parking lot after switching its plates with those of a nearby Honda Accord. There was no University, at least not physically—there was merely a PO box and bank account and a phone number that redirected to a voice message stating that the University of Chesterson's financial aid office was closed but please try again tomorrow morning, and of course only the address was necessary, but it didn't hurt to pay attention to the details. If the big things—the marriage and the access to Lydia's student and financial information that the marriage afforded and the fabricated identity and the fake university address—were the building blocks of the long con, then the little things, the details—the baby and the phone number and months of counseling sessions—were the cement. Much like the University of Chesterson, Gary Pelletier didn't actually exist. His real name was Raul Vega Gonzales, and he was thirty-three years old when he'd met Lydia McCormick at a party and when she'd told him all about herself and her $50,000 government scholarship and when he'd gotten her drunk and when he'd slipped a capsule of gamma-Hydroxybutyric acid into her light beer and when he'd taken her to bed and impregnated her and then married her. And a year after that he was quite a good deal wealthier—enough that he could float for a couple years, get by on the short cons—and halfway across Arizona in a stolen Chrysler LeBaron.

Lydia's scholarship money was gone and the bank account she'd shared with her husband withdrawn, and even as she filed the police report and spoke to financial aid officials who in turn spoke to the facilitators of the Maxine Bridwell Honors Scholarship Program, set up in the honor of the late Maxine Bridwell, a very wealthy California educator, politician, and philanthropist, it was explained to her that, even though she was the victim of fraud, that was it. There was no more money for her, and of course she could continue studying at UCSD, but she would have to pay for it. There were grants and loan programs she could apply for if she wanted, especially some very generous ones focused on assisting single mothers interested in pursuing higher education, but she'd at the very least have to sit out the semester, and possibly the entire year, while she waited for approval, which by the way had every chance of being denied. And then also, the police told her, they couldn't rule out the possibility that she'd been in league with her husband in the whole thing, that they'd collaborated in an effort to defraud the California government and the Maxine Bridwell estate and UCSD. There would be an extensive investigation.

And so Lydia, now again Lydia McCormick—although she wasn't sure which name was worse, her mother's or her fake husband's—moved into a tiny apartment in Encanto with her now four-month-old son and got a job first at a small diner and then as a secretary at a used car dealership where the owner, a disgusting man with bad hair, made sure Lydia was well-paid in exchange for certain favors. Ambitions of returning to school melted away slowly, one month at a time, until they no longer existed at all, and she even played around with certain soft drugs for a while while raising her child alone.

Scott returned to The Grill's Youngstown, Ohio, location on Tuesday just as he'd been asked. It was a beautiful day—bright and sunny and just a few white puffy clouds dotting the sky here and there—and Scott had seen on the news that morning that the temperature would be around eighty degrees, and he knew it must have been close to that already because his brow was sweaty and his thick black hair, which he'd combed back before leaving the house, was now hanging chaotically in front of his eyes, a few of the looser strands sticking to the sweat on his forehead, and the sweat even ran into his eyes a bit, burning his retinas or corneas or whichever one the white part was called. And he blinked and rubbed his eyes, and they felt better, and he pulled a folded grey handkerchief out of his right back pocket and dabbed it against his forehead. He was wearing a brand new pair of black Docker-style off-brand trousers, on which he'd spent seventeen of his last fifty dollars, and which already had flecks of mud speckled along the bottom near the cuffs because he'd, being carless, walked the twenty minutes to work, but he'd enjoyed the walk because it was such a beautiful day. He wore shoes that he'd had for years —he'd first purchased them when he started working at Charlie's over in Niles, Ohio, what like six years ago now?, and he'd worn them the entire time he'd worked there and continued to wear them when he quit Charlie's and started working at Groovy Burger, and he'd taken them with him to Pittsburgh and worn them the seven-or-so months he'd worked at the Pittsburgh Groovy Burger—and so they'd seen better days for sure, what with the rubber sole beginning to peel off and the tread having worn down noticeably and a few of the seams visibly slipshod and worn, but he kept them and still wore them, even to this new job at The Grill, because a really good pair of black non-slip work shoes can be expensive, and if he'd purchased new pants *and* new shoes, he'd have very little —like less than ten dollars—left until he received his first tips at this new job, which wouldn't be until after he'd completed training, so like several days or a week. His shirt was older too, but still in excellent condition, and it was a black polo-style shirt with three buttons and a collar, and it fit well, showing off the lean muscular physique he'd developed slowly over the last couple years. His belt was also black, just as he'd been instructed, but his socks were argyle with spots of red and blue, because he'd decided a long time ago to never again wear socks that were plain white or plain black because he'd never met a person who did so who was truly all that interesting.

It was 8:55 AM when Scott walked up to and along the side of the brownish-tannish brick-and-vinyl building with the words THE GRILL in big red curved letters on the top, making his way to the front. He approached the large glass double doors, which were actually part of an airlock-style system wherein there were two doors on the outside, and then a small atrium with short benches and potted plants against the sides and news clippings about The Grill framed on the wall, and then two more large glass double doors on the inside, leading into the open restaurant lobby with more benches—these ones padded—and a couple more plants in tall, dark green planters. Most restaurants had this sort of double-double-door system, and Scott assumed it was to keep things like leaves and garbage from blowing into the lobby when customers entered and exited the building. As he approached the first set of glass doors, he reached out and pulled the handle on the left door, but the door didn't swing outward or otherwise move, and so he shifted his grip to the one on the right, but that door seemed to be locked as well. He rapped his hand lightly on the glass. There was no movement inside the building.

And so he turned and stood, his arms folded across his chest, watching the parking lot for a few minutes until a black four-door Chrysler Sebring pulled in from the busy street and passed Scott by and drove around toward the back of the building. Scott followed and watched as the car pulled into a spot not far from the dumpsters. It idled for a few seconds before Geoff McCree turned off the ignition, got out, and closed the driver-side door behind him. He was wearing faded jeans and a blue and yellow jacket. Scott recognized the sports team the colors represented, but thought that the very fact the man was wearing a jacket today was absurd.

"Whew," Geoff said, and Scott noticed that his face, like Scott's, was matted with sweat. "Sorry I'm late—I honestly didn't think you would be here on time. Nobody's ever here on time. Here, let's go in this way." He gestured for Scott to follow and walked around to the front of the building, where Scott had been waiting earlier. He pulled out a keychain with what looked like dozens of keys on it and unlocked one of the doors. He opened it but didn't hold it open for Scott and walked inside, and Scott followed him. Geoff didn't say anything; he just walked through the lobby, which was warm and stuffy and open to the rest of the restaurant, and around the chest-high wall that separated the hostess station from the bar area, and so Scott followed him back that way and watched as Geoff turned on one of the bar televisions and changed the channel to ESPN and then walked up to a series of switches and dials and knobs on the wall and turned one of the knobs marked AIR all the way to the right, and Scott assumed that the knob controlled the air conditioner, and he was pretty sure that he was right because almost immediately the atmosphere inside the restaurant began to lose its stuffiness. "Here," Geoff finally said. "Have a seat over at this booth here, and I'll go get the orientation stuff. Would you like something to drink? I'm going to make coffee."

"Coffee sounds good," Scott said graciously, and Geoff asked if he wanted cream or sugar and Scott said no. Geoff asked if Scott was sure, and Scott said yes, he was sure. Geoff disappeared through a set of wooden swinging double doors; the left one was marked NO and the right one YES, both in large white block letters. Geoff had briefly pushed at the left one with futility before walking through the right.

Scott sat in the booth that Geoff had indicated—the same booth where they'd sat a few days ago during his interview—and waited for the man to return. The bar a few feet away from Scott was shaped like a horseshoe, with barstools running all the way around it, except that the part of a horseshoe that would normally be open was in this case closed off, a complete wall with a glassless window and a small surface where Scott assumed the bartender would place drinks for the servers to pick up, an assumption that was further confirmed by the presence of a computer monitor just above the window. The rest of the wall was covered from floor to ceiling with dozens of different bottles —a few different brands each of bourbon, vodka, gin, tequila, and other spirits; a scotch or two; several different schnapps; and at least a dozen different kinds of wine. Scott was impressed with the variety–if the drink selection was any indication, he would be proud to serve the food The Grill made. Scott noted that the ambiance of the bar, which was located in almost the exact center of the restaurant, was rather dark, the dim lights casting a soft, comfortable glow on the surrounding booths, and that the restaurant became brighter around its edges, outside the bar area, where there were many floor-to-ceiling windows letting in the natural light from outside, diffused only slightly through sets of wooden blinds.

Geoff reappeared, this time coming out of the NO door, and Scott surmised that the purpose of the YES and the NO must be to prevent collisions as busy waiters and waitresses moved in and out of the kitchen, and therefore the NO door probably said YES on the other side, and similarly the YES door NO. In Geoff's arms was a large stack of papers and training manuals and in his left hand a single cup of coffee, which spilled a little onto the table and the papers as Geoff set it down. Geoff was no longer wearing the blue and yellow jacket.

"First," Geoff said, as he sat down and sipped from the coffee, and as Scott immediately gave up hope of getting any coffee himself, "I need you to fill this out." He slid a sheet of paper across the table along with a cheap blue ballpoint pen, and Scott began to fill out the paper with his personal information: full name, phone number, social security number—all of this information was on his application, and Scott was sure that Geoff could easily have copied it from that and saved him the trouble. When Scott had finished with this sheet, Geoff gave him some more papers to fill out and sign, including tax forms and safety forms and forms confirming that Scott was, indeed, a legal resident of the United States and neither an illegal immigrant nor a convicted felon, at least not a felon who had been convicted within the last twelve months, and even if he was, the paper said, that didn't necessarily preclude him from employment.

Scott filled in all the necessary papers and gave them back to Geoff, and Geoff set them aside and slid across the table a thick white, spiral-bound tome, the title of which read:

"THE GRILL" TRAINING MANUAL: REQUIREMENTS AND EXPECTATIONS OF EXCELLENCE FOR FOH (FRONT OF THE HOUSE) EMPLOYEES

"I'm supposed to go over this with you," Geoff said, "and then you're supposed to sign this paper saying that I went over it with you and that you understood everything."

It took them a little over half-an-hour to go through the whole manual, which Geoff essentially just read to Scott as Scott read along. The manual contained all the information to which Scott had become accustomed to seeing in restaurant training manuals: a brief history of the company, the company's mission statement (which, as mission statements tended to be, was both trite and contrived), uniform guidelines, procedures for responsible alcohol service, social networking policies, guest treatment protocols, etc., and the clear declaration that the violation of any of the policies herein would result in disciplinary action "up to and including termination." By the time they had finished, and after Scott had signed the paper confirming that he'd been guided through and fully understood the company policies, it was nearly ten o'clock.

"We open for lunch at eleven," Geoff said, "and I want to have you out of here by then, so for today I'm just going to show you the orientation video, and you can start the computer training next time. Follow me." Geoff led him out of the bar area and over to a table near the windows. As he followed, Scott saw a large man, a genuinely *fat* man, in a white chef's uniform enter through the front door and walk back into the kitchen. "Here, sit here," Geoff said, gesturing to the table, which was long and had eight chairs positioned around it. "I'm going to go get the TV."

Scott sat in the chair idly. He contemplated whistling.

Geoff returned several minutes later awkwardly carrying a 21-inch tube-style television with built-in DVD- and VHS-players. Geoff plugged the TV into a socket on the wall behind the table and turned it on. He took a remote from his pocket, and Scott knew he must have hit the INPUT or VIDEO button, because the static on the screen was suddenly replaced by a colorful DVD menu. "Here." He handed the remote to Scott. "I've got to go get things ready for lunch and stuff, so I'll be in the kitchen or the office if you need anything. Oh, and hey, do you want something to drink? Coffee or something?"

The following is a transcript of the orientation video, which was clearly filmed on VHS and transferred to a digital format at a later date, that was shown to Scott Pelletier during his first day of training at The Grill. Copyright, Earl's American Grill Restaurant Group, Inc. 2007:

[EARL E. BRADFORD, JR.] Well howdy thar. Mah name is Earl E. Bradford, the second, an' ahm the CEO of The Grill. Ahm here taday to tell y'all about the fine comp'ny far which you've dacided to start workin'. First, le' me assure ya that, in dahsiden to start workin' for this fine comp'ny, you've made prolly the best, most fine dahsision ya e'er made. Because here at The Grill, we b'lieve in excellence, an' we accept nothin' less than excellence. When ah started this comp'ny in 1973 with mah late brother, Theodore Bradford, ah knew that ah wanted to create a place where ar guests could come an' si'down and order tha' finest, most succulent burgers an' the finest, most delicious steaks at a price that's both affordable an' profitable. But it weren't jus' about the food when ah started—when mah brother an' ah started, that is—this restaurant: We were, an' still are, here at The Grill, committed to given' ar customers—guests, that is—the finest, most relaxed an' comfortable atmosphere ya can find in a casual fine dining restaurant. An' this is where y'all come in. But first, before we get in t'all that, ahm gonna let Jennifer Bell, ar senior vice president of marketing an' guest relations, tell you a lil' bit 'bout the h'st'ry of this fine comp'ny. Take it away, Jennifer.

[JENNIFER BELL, chuckling] Thanks, Earl.

In the fall of 1973 [A SERIES OF BLACK AND WHITE PICTURES—EVEN THOUGH COLORED FILM EXISTED IN 1973—OF A YOUNG EARL E. BRADFORD BEGINS TO PLAY ACROSS THE SCREEN WHILE JENNIFER BELL SPEAKS], Earl E. Bradford Jr., then a recent graduate of the University of Austin [*SIC* — THE COLLEGE'S NAME IS ACTUALLY "THE UNIVERSITY OF TEXAS AT AUSTIN," AND SAID UNIVERSITY'S WEBSITE SPORTS A PICTURE OF A HEAD OF LETTUCE OR SOMETHING FOR SOME REASON] in Austin, Texas, opened his first restaurant with his brother, Theodore S. Bradford, and the duo called the restaurant "Earl and Teddy's American Grill." In fact, this original location, at 5334 South Main Street, is still in operation today, only two blocks from the company's national headquarters.

The goal that Teddy and Earl Bradford had for this restaurant was a simple one: provide the people of Austin with the best burgers and steaks in town while also giving them a place where they could just hang out and relax and feel like family. With its rich, mahogany tables, its high ceilings and low-hanging chandelier-style light fixtures, its unique arcade area, and its large and fully stocked bar, Earl and Teddy's American Grill accomplished just that. A popular end-of-the-day destination for college students, businessmen, and even local families, the restaurant started bringing in record profits in record time, and in the summer of 1974, only eight months after opening their first store, Earl and Theodore Bradford opened their second location in nearby Buda, Texas, and their burgers became a staple at the annual Buda Wiener Dog Races. Within two-and-a-half years of opening their first restaurant, Earl and Theodore Bradford opened a total of eleven restaurants, and by

1980, Earl and Teddy's American Grill had expanded to over one-hundred-and-fifty locations in 25 states.

And then, in July of 1982, tragedy struck the Bradford family. On a stormy summer night, Earl and Teddy Bradford, along with their parents, Eline and Earl Bradford, Sr., were on their way to Teddy's wedding in Spain when their private jet was struck by lightning. Earl Sr., who was an accomplished pilot and World War II Air Force veteran and was flying the plane that day, attempted a water landing in the Atlantic off the coast of Sicily. Everyone aboard the plane, except for Earl Jr., was killed.

After spending months in a coma, Bradford awoke to find his restaurant empire even stronger than before the accident, having come under the default control of Elsa Marie Esparanza, Theodore Bradford's fiancé. There followed a love story born of tragedy, and on February 11, 1983, Earl and Elsa married in a private ceremony.

As the years passed, Earl and Teddy's American Grill experienced continuous record-breaking success, growing to become, by 1997, America's fifth-largest casual fine dining chain.

In 2002, though, Earl decided it was time for a change, and he began to re-imagine the way in which consumers would experience dining going forward. A visionary in his own right, Earl Bradford knew that the world was changing: gone were the days when customers were content with just a burger and fries and a couple of hours playing arcade-style video games that had long since become outdated. And so Bradford set about remodeling all 800-plus stores, removing the arcades and updating the menu with fresh, high-quality items to reflect a more modern taste. And because the chain had long ago expanded into both Mexico and Canada, as well as nine other countries, the company was renamed, and with that, The Grill, as it's called today, was born.

[EARL E. BRADFORD, JR.] And that's perty much it, really. Quite a story, ain't it? An' ah couldn't be more proud of this comp'ny and the fine people that have had a part in its success. But waddas this mean for you?

Well, as a new member of The Grill family, you have the won'erful pervlige of upholding the name an' reputation . . .

[The contents of a large portion of the orientation video are unknown, because at this point, Scott Pelletier had to take a leak, and so he got up and went to the bathroom and left the DVD playing. Eventually, he returned.]

[UNRECOGNIZED NARRATOR, NEITHER EARL E. BRADFORD, JR. NOR JENNIFER BELL] . . . and so with items like these—premium fork-tender steaks and burgers made with the highest-quality Angus beef and seafood dishes like our popular Surf-and-Turf, Honey-glazed Grilled Jumbo Shrimp, and giant All-you-can-crack King Crab Legs—there's no denying that The Grill has the most diverse and satisfying menus of any casual fine dining restaurant.

[EARL E. BRADFORD, JR.] Well, then, that's it for now. As ya continya ta train, ya'll learn more an' more about this fine comp'ny, an ahm confadent that ya'll be jus' as proud ta be a member a The Grill family as ah am, and as ah know my brother Teddy Bradford would be if he were still alive today. Thank ya, and good luck on your journey with this fine comp'ny.

* * *

After he watched the orientation video, Scott stood up and wandered toward the back of the restaurant, looking for Geoff and wondering if, since he had finished the video and everything, he should just leave, because Geoff had told him that the store would be opening at eleven and it was ten-forty-three right now, but then he realized that he didn't know what day or time he was supposed to come back to continue training, so he decided to continue looking for Geoff until he found him.

In restaurants, especially American chain restaurants, there is a certain dichotomy that exists between the front of the house (FOH) and the back of the house (BOH). The FOH, which is generally accepted to comprise the dining room, the bar, the lobby or foyer, and even the men's and women's customer restrooms, which in almost every single restaurant have two stalls and two urinals—or in the women's case just two stalls—and a large mirror above a longish counter area with two inset sinks and two paper towel dispensers or those metal under- or over-powered hot air hand dryers and a trash can and a baby changing station and floor made of thousands of tiny little tiles in a pattern of alternating colors like blue-green-blue or maroon-darkgreen-maroon or offwhite-maroon-offwhite-darkblue-offwhite-maroon and smells not exactly bad but certainly not good like maybe the restroom has just been in operation for too many years and no amount of air-freshener can quite do the job, is usually clean and open and tidy yet dark, and this is reflected in everything, from the lamps and lampshades to the wood finish, which has worn significantly, giving it not a trashy but a vintage look; from the clothes the FOH employees—hostesses, managers, servers, bartenders—wear, to the clothes that even the customers wear. The BOH on the other hand, which is also often collectively called "the kitchen," especially by those unfamiliar with the restaurant industry, comprises a whole slew of areas, including the grill station, the fryer and broil station, the prep line, the dish area, the dry storage room, the walk-in cooler, the freezer, and, as a sort of walk-in-within-a-walk-in, the beer cooler, which is usually locked and accessible only to managerial staff out of a usually unfounded fear that some entrepreneurial employee is going to break in and take cases and kegs of ales and lagers—most restaurants, especially American chain restaurants, rarely serve stouts—and make off with them somehow and sneak them out the back door without anybody else seeing. In direct contrast to the FOH, the BOH tends towards bright and crowded and grimy and cluttered and dirty. So Scott, who had worked at two or three restaurants before this one (he fluctuated between counting and discounting his first job, which was as a busser at a Bob Evans for six months when he was sixteen), was unsurprised and even a little sated when he pushed open one of the doors with the word YES on it and walked back into the kitchen and found it better lit than the dining room and noted the bits of food and paper—napkins and receipts and slips from order pads—and pieces of silverware strewn about the floor's brown tiles and gathered in piles at the base of the garbage cans.

To the right of the swinging doors through which Scott had entered was a long metal countertop equipped with two soda fountains, a coffee pot, a shelf stacked with about a dozen serving trays, and racks and racks of tall clear glasses and white coffee cups. Scott immediately recognized the server aisle—or the service prep area or the serving station or whatever the term they used here was—that strange almost interdimensional amalgamation of FOH and BOH aesthetics, both clean and cluttered, sterile and dirty, dark and light. Across from and directly parallel to the service station, separated from it by six or so feet of the brown tile, was another countertop, this one more like a shelf, and above it was another long shelf with heating coils, and behind this whole structure was the fat man in the white chef's uniform setting up what was clearly the grill/fry/broil station.

The fat man—it wasn't that Scott was judging, just that the man was in fact fat and had no other defining features—was the only person around, and so Scott said, "Excuse me. Have you seen Geoff?"

The man, holding a sort of paintbrush in one hand and an amber container of cooking oil in the other, looked up from what he was doing, which was applying the oil generously to the surface of the grill. "You new?"

"Yeah. It's my first day of training. Orientation, really."

"'S'your name?"

"Scott."

"Hey, Scott, I'm Joe, and I think Geoff's in the office."

"Thanks." Scott looked around. He saw the service station and the pass and the grill area, and across the room by the other set of swinging doors was the dish station and the large dishwashing apparatus. "Hey," he said with a humility he didn't often show, "where is the office?"

Joe grinned, and Scott realized that, for a cook, Joe was a nice guy. "Back there, right past the prep area and the cooler."

"Thanks."

And so Scott walked past the dish station where Joe the cook had pointed, and there was the prep station, a large open area with a table and three sinks against the wall and a stove with two large pots that looked like maybe they were for heating soup —"heating" is the correct term here, for in Scott's experience, restaurants that were part of casual American dining chains never actually *cooked* their soup, but rather the soup was shipped to them all ready to go in gallon-sized bags, and they just had to put the bags in large pots of hot water for a while—and two refrigerators and an ice machine. Just beyond the prep station, kind of around the corner from the grill area, Scott saw the large metal door of the walk-in cooler, and next to that a door with a window through which he saw Geoff and a computer and a filing cabinet, and next to that door there was another door with a sign on it that said DRY STORAGE.

Scott walked up to the office door and tapped on it lightly with his knuckles. Geoff turned around and saw him and opened the door. "Finished with the video?"

Scott nodded. "Is that it for today? I didn't know when you wanted me to come in next."

Geoff turned around and pulled a spreadsheet up on the computer, on which Scott could see a list of names and times. "Yeah, hmmm. Yeah. Come in . . ." Geoff scratched his head and Scott stepped back a little as bits of dandruff were flung into the air ". . . come in tomorrow at the same time, the same time as today, and we'll get you started on the computer, and then maybe I'll have you follow Michelle around or something for a while."

Scott didn't know who Michelle was, but he said that sounded good and he would be here tomorrow, then.

"Oh, and wait," Geoff said. He moved his hand up to the collar of his shirt and pinched it and kind of tugged at it. "Your shirt. You need to wear like more of a, like more of a t-shirt, not like a polo like that. It can't have a collar like that. It still needs to be black, though, and short sleeved like that one, it just can't have a collar like that."

Scott nodded and said okay, but he wondered what could possibly be wrong with a black polo shirt, since weren't polos nicer than t-shirts, anyway? Weren't collars supposed to be a good thing, fashionably speaking?

The girl with the blonde hair was named Lori Bristol. She smiled as she opened the door, her large red purse draped over her arm at the elbow and a hot low-fat caramel latte with whipped cream in her hand, and the new guy walked toward her. Her smile disappeared because he seemed to not even see her, and he just walked right on by, not even acknowledging her or that she'd held the door for him. His face was kind of screwed up in a thoughtful expression, she noticed, his lips thin but tight and his eyebrows not exactly furled but tilted inward a little.

Lori shrugged and smiled again, to herself this time, and took a sip of her latte and burned her tongue.

Nine Months Pre Brand-Changing Day, 2012

For most restaurants in most cities, Friday night is the busiest shift of the week. It is, after all, the start of the weekend, and a whole wealth of factors—children don't have school in the morning; parents don't have work; paychecks have been cashed; and others—seem to conspire against the American Server, who of course works on Friday night and therefore is not among the throngs flocking to dine out. It's something of an irony for the American Server, though, a sort of two-edged sword that becomes just a little bit démodé after only so many weeks: Fridays are the busiest and so by all conceivable logic should be the most profitable—and they're plenty profitable for the American Restaurant, let there be no mistake—but there's a certain threshold of customers at which the quality of service any one human person is able to provide begins to take a noticeable hit.

Scott had learned last week that The Grill was no different, that management—and whether this was rooted at the local level or in corporate philosophy he'd not yet made a judgement on, but would guess both—seemed to value the restaurant's income more than the individuals'. And that's why he winced when he heard the call behind him.

"Excuse me. Excuse me, waiter."

He recognized the voice immediately as that of the thirty-something lady with bleach-blonde hair and unnaturally tanned skin who was with a gentleman she probably met on some internet dating website and had just tonight met in person for the first time and, unbeknownst to her but obvious to those dining around her, was failing miserably to impress. "Excuuuuuse me," she said again, drawing out the letter U like a small child craving attention.

Scott was carrying three very hot plates—one in each hand and the third balanced with considerable skill on his right forearm—and he'd just walked by the lady with the bleach-blonde hair, so he knew she must have seen this and should have ascertained that he was delivering meals to another customer. He would have just continued walking, ignored the woman, pretended he hadn't heard her, and delivered the food and taken care of other customers and caught the bleach-blonde woman on the way back, but he'd sort of flinched involuntarily the first time she'd called out, his back had sort of stiffened and he'd inhaled a sharp, shallow breath, so he knew that she had called for him, and she knew that he knew, and he knew that she knew that he knew, so he had no choice but to turn around—slowly, keeping his arms straight and steady—and face her with his sincerest artificial smile. "Yes?" he said. "How is everything? Can I get you something?"

The woman held up a breadbasket and her empty cocktail glass. "We need more breadsticks," she said.

Her date's eyes were wide and his top lip stuck out over the bottom in a frown.

"And could I get another strawberry margarita?"

"Of course," Scott said, the smile still fixed firmly on his face. "Just a moment." He was going to turn around, but the woman actually tried to hand him the empty margarita glass, and despite the plates in his hands and on his arm, he reflexively tried to reach for it.

Scott had never, in the four years he'd been waiting tables, dropped a plate of food. He'd dropped glasses, even spilled an entire large water on a customer once—which customer was very upset and very wet and demanded not only a free meal but also a dry change of clothes, and fortunately this had happened at a Groovy Burger, and Groovy Burger sold these green and black Groovy Burger t-shirts with anagrams on them like "Voorgy Gruber" and "Grub Over Gyro" and "Rob Grover Guy" (which was especially funny because the Groovy Burger's manager was named Rob Guy, but his middle name wasn't Grover) and even "Rub Grove Orgy," so they were able to give the guy at least a clean dry shirt, and Scott had been reprimanded because those shirts aren't cheap, you know—and he had even dropped an entire tray of dirty dishes in the BOH, but he'd never actually dropped a plate that still had a customer's undelivered food on it, and so his brain started to freak out, like spazz even, as the plate on his forearm wobbled precariously. And then the plate started to slide from his arm, and it was like a lame action movie where everything was happening in slow motion but what was happening wasn't all that interesting so what was the director thinking slowing everything down *now?* Scott held his breath, and it felt like the bleach-blonde lady might have been holding her breath, might even have realized that this was all her fault, and her date was certainly holding his breath, and if the restaurant were a biological organism, it might have been holding its breath, too. And the plate fell, it actually fell, and on it was a perfectly cooked medium-rare ribeye and garlic mashed potatoes and grilled green beans and a side of A-1 sauce, and the small cup of A-1 sauce toppled off the plate and onto the floor, and the sauce itself ejaculated from the cup and spread itself out across three feet of carpet and even managed to land on a couple of chair legs. And the plate followed the cup of A-1, but then it didn't, because a hand appeared suddenly and caught it and steadied it and took it from him. Scott, whose heart was pounding, actually pounding, said, "Thanks."

Lori smiled at him and winked and said, "Sure thing, sweet cheeks. Now where's this going?"

Scott smiled too and said, "Table 49."

Lori took also the plate from his left hand and started for table 49. Scott watched her go, the third and final plate still in his right hand, and made a mental note to get more A-1, and the bleach-blonde woman gave Scott the margarita glass and said, "And don't forget: more breadsticks, too."

There were twelve servers on the floor on this particular Friday night, which sounds like a lot but still isn't enough when your restaurant doesn't have an official wait policy and so is technically required to seat every incoming guest here and now no matter what and so each server might have seven or eight tables at a time, which *is* a lot.

Scott, of course, was working tonight, and this was his second Friday night shift at The Grill since he'd finished his training a few weeks ago. He currently had five tables, but he was next in the rotation to be sat, "sat" being the term the American Server uses to describe getting a new table of customers. Scott liked to joke that getting sat was just one step away from getting laid. He'd even made the joke to Lori, who was also one of the twelve servers on the floor tonight (laid on the floor, get it?) and who was so far something of a conundrum for Scott. She was beautiful, her hair blonde and curled tightly, and possibly the most intelligent of all the women who worked here. She flirted with Scott like crazy, like she *really* flirted with him, said some downright dirty things, but she also had a boyfriend and was nineteen years old and also talked a hell of a lot about Jesus, and everyone told Scott that she was pretty devout in her faith.

Scott stood at the back of the dining room near one of the POS (point of sale) systems trying to ring in bleach-blonde's third strawberry margarita. *Trying* because the damn touch screen needed calibrating—it was one of those resistive touch screens that require that the user actually *press down* on the screen, sometimes rather forcefully, before it would register the touch, rather than the capacitive kind, which only needs an electrical signal, like that from a fingertip, in order to register the touch, and even though the capacitive ones work better, the resistive touch screens are cheaper and liquid-resistant, so restaurants tend to use them, even though Scott had never actually seen anyone spill liquid on a POS—and so when he tried to press the key for strawberry margarita, which was actually labeled and advertised as a "Strawberry Grillarita" (cute) the POS repeatedly registered it as a Mango Tango Flamingo Grillarita, which, yes, actually is one of the drinks available at The Grill and is made with mango chunks, orange juice, tequila and garnished with a lime and a little pink plastic stick with a flamingo on the end. After the fourth try, Scott gave up and logged out of the system and then logged back in, and this time the POS registered his touch correctly. There's a reason the American Server wryly thinks of POS as an acronym for Piece of Shit.

Just as Scott hit the SEND ORDER key, Kara Green

appeared beside him, intercepting control of the computer as soon as he'd finished with it, which interception was necessary when there were twelve servers on the floor and only four working POS interfaces in the dining room (there were six total, but the screens of two of them had stopped working months ago), and began typing in an order of her own. "They need to turn the air on in here," she said without moving her focus from the screen. "It's hotter than a whore in church. I should know."

Scott crinkled his nose. "I don't—"

"Wait!" Kara started laughing. She turned from the screen and faced Scott, placed her hand on his shoulder, and looked up at him. "Damn, I totally screwed that up. Wait wait wait wait wait. Okay okay, let me try that again."

Scott waved his hand in a *go for it* sort of gesture.

"Okay okay." Kara stood tall, straightened her back and puffed her chest and cleared her throat. "They need to turn the air on in here. I'm sweating worse than a whore in church."

"Ah," Scott said. "That does make more sense."

"And I should know." Kara Green was Scott's age—Scott actually knew her from like way back in kindergarten or first grade before she'd moved to a different school, which took them almost a week of working together to realize. She was a single mom now, having been knocked up (her words) a couple of years ago, but she was doing okay and even owned a house, and her mother helped take care of her daughter when she was at work and school, where she was finishing up courses on finance or tax auditing or something. Scott liked her, and he sort of wanted to sleep with her, but just for sex, and he wasn't sure if that would ever actually happen. She turned back to the screen and continued ringing in her order.

* * *

In the office, way in the back of the BOH, just around the corner from the prep area, with the door closed and sports-focused talk radio emanating from his phone's tiny speakers, the phone being plugged into its charger, which he had brought with him today because it was Friday and he not only opened this morning but would be sticking around until 8:00 PM or so in case any problems popped up before letting R.J., who was actually here now and keeping an eye on the FOH, take over for the rest of the shift and oversee the closers, Geoff McCree typed away at the office computer, which was an old p.o.s. (piece of shit) that still ran Windows XP even now in 2012 and whose screen resolution hurt your eyes to look at for any extended period of time. The only sound besides the talk radio and Geoff's heavy breathing—the BOH AC had stopped working yesterday —was the clack clack clackity clack of the keyboard as Geoff typed out a requisition order for a new Alto-Shaam fryer because the kitchen's Alto-Shaam fryer had stopped working two days ago, leaving the cooks with only two fryers that held only two baskets each instead of three fryers that held two baskets each, reducing the total number of fryer baskets that could be used at any given time to four baskets down from the usual six. Geoff had done the math himself.

It's a well-known and widely accepted fact among cocktail enthusiasts that one should never order certain drinks from the bar of an American chain restaurant unless one intends to instruct the so-called bartender precisely how to make it. Margaritas, for example, are by default almost never made to the official specifications of the International Bartender's Association, which stipulates that a standard margarita be made with fifty percent tequila, twenty-nine percent Cointreau-brand triple sec, and twenty-one percent fresh-squeezed lime juice and served over fresh, whole ice cubes. At The Grill, however, a margarita is made by taking a stereotypical margarita glass, which is actually a Champagne coupe, salting the rim, and holding the glass under the dispenser of a professional-grade margarita machine. The bartender then pulls the lever at the top of the dispenser and fills the glass with a ready-made frozen margarita mix composed of a number of different ingredients including tequila, water, corn syrup, sugar, citric acid, natural flavors, sodium citrate, sodium benzoate and potassium sorbate (to preserve flavor), cellulose gum, polysorbate 60, gum arabic, glycerol abietate and FD&C yellow no. 5; an additional fruit mix is then added, depending on which Grillarita the guest has ordered. This is the standard at all of the chain's locations, except for stores in Hawaii, and except for the Mango Tango Grillarita, which is actually made fresh and with fresh ingredients.

Bleach-blonde, Scott noted, was clearly not a cocktail connoisseur at any level and rather just liked alcohol. She was currently very drunk—even though Scott had cut her off after three drinks, she had managed to circumvent him by ordering directly from Mike, the bartender, who wasn't aware that she'd already been served—and her date had left her some time ago. She sat in her booth alone, sobbing quietly. She was the only person in this half of the restaurant, the section now closed and the last of Scott's guests having left upwards of thirty minutes ago.

"What should we do?" Scott said, his voice low.

"I don't *know*," Lori said, her voice also barely above a

whisper, even though they stood six tables away from Bleach-blonde's lonely booth-like hallow of inebriation and self-pity. "Why are you asking *me*? I don't *drink*."

"Stop that," Scott said.

"Stop *what*?"

"*That.* That right there — you keep emphasizing the last word of your sentences."

"*So?*"

"So, it's annoying."

"You think I'm annoying?"

"No, I don't think you're annoying. I mean, I don't know you very well, but I think you're rather great so far. It's just your inflection that's annoying. So, anyway, what should we do about Bleach-blonde over there?"

"Bleach-blonde?"

"Yeah, it's what I've been calling her all night in my head."

"Why Bleach-blonde? You have something against blondes?"

Scott sighed. "No, of course not. You're blonde. No. It's just that she's, you know . . . stereotypical and all. Look at her."

"I don't know what you're talking about."

"Well, you haven't been the one waiting on her for the last two hours."

"So you think my inflection is annoying."

Scott sighed again.

"I think you're lying. I think you think my inflection is sexy."

"I think your inflection is sexy as hell," Scott couldn't help flirting. With any woman, really, but especially with Lori.

"You think I'm sexy."

Scott sighed again. "Bleach-blonde?"

"Yeah. Well—and stop calling her that—we can't let her drive home. I guess we should call her a cab."

"Do we even have cabs in Youngstown?"

"Yeah, we must have cabs. I mean, we have to have cabs, right? How else do drunk people get home?"

"I've never seen a cab around here."

"We're a city. Cities have cabs."

"Youngstown isn't much of a city."

"We should just tell R.J."

"That Youngstown is a shitty city?"

"That your customer is drunk."

"Yes. I suppose that's a good idea."

They found R.J. standing near kitchen doors, arms folded, looking over the dining room like a watchful sultan. He told them that, yes, there were cabs in Youngstown, and that they actually had to call them for intoxicated customers more often than one would think.

"I told you there are cabs in Youngstown," Lori whispered as they walked back to Scott's section.

"Damn."

"Hey, just because I'm sexy doesn't mean I can't be right—"

"*Dammit.*"

"Hey, what—?"

Scott put his hands on her shoulders, turned her, gently, trying to ignore the sensation of his hands on her skin, about thirty degrees to her left, and pointed toward Bleach-blonde's booth, which was unoccupied and covered in vomit.

"Ah. Yes, damn." Lori said.

R.J. had always hated Fridays. In fact, routinely through his mind on Friday nights did pass the thought: *I hate Friday.* Recently, though, he'd begun to hate not just Fridays, but also every other day. Whereas before he was content to tolerate just about everything, he'd become convinced that apathy was terrible sin, and so now he tended to passionately despise most people and also his job and just about everything, so that now a more common thought was: *I hate it all.*

It was this thought that he thought as the two servers walked away—Lori whose name he knew and the new guy whose name he hadn't felt like learning yet but knew he eventually would.

R.J. grunted. If there was an intoxicated customer in the building, he was supposed to let Geoff know, so he turned around and shoved the kitchen door hard with his forearm and headed for the office.

Because the AC had stopped working in the BOH, and he had neglected all day to turn it on in the FOH, Geoff had placed three large fans, the industrial-sized fans that are really big and made of all metal and sit on the floor, around the BOH—one at the end of the grill/fry/broil area so that it faced the line cooks, another in the prep area, and the third sort of in between the pass and server station and the dish station, where it didn't really do anybody any good; in fact, the breeze generated by a server opening one of the doors was cooler and more effectively directed. There was not, however, a fan in the office, not even a small desk fan or a tall standing fan, because the office was maybe five feet by five feet and the big fans just wouldn't fit and there were no small fans in the building, and Geoff couldn't find the time to buy one for like fifteen bucks. He kept the door closed because that was policy—the office door was supposed to be closed at all times, save of course for when someone was entering or exiting. And plus also Geoff was wearing his jacket still because he had been doing the meat counts in the walk-in maybe an hour ago and had forgotten to take it off. And that's why when R.J. found him at around 7:00 PM, Geoff had passed out due to mild heat stroke. But it was okay because the doctors cooled him down, and he insisted on returning to work the very next day, such was what he called his "passion" for the job.

Eight Months Pre Brand-Changing Day, 2012

Scott's head, face, hands, feet, and chest were numb. He blinked and blinked and blinked again. He shook his head left and right. He asked for a glass of water, realized he'd already asked for one and it had already been placed before him on the table. He picked it up, raised it to his mouth and hit his teeth hard, except not as hard as it felt like he had hit them. He course-corrected, gulped the water. It didn't help. His body still hurt and his mouth was dry.

"You're drunk."

Kara said this. And she said it loudly, too, yelled it really, because the music threatened to drown out her words otherwise, and she was still coherent enough to understand this.

"I am not," Scott said, his voice sloppy and drenched in protest and booze.

"Oh, real—?"

"*Drunk. Drunk!*" Scott said. "I'm not *drunk*. I was going. To say. Drunk but you didn't let me finish my sentence so I didn't get to say it. Drunk. I didn't get to say it. I didn't get to say drunk."

The music, a techno-pop-rock-Saturday-night-dance-remix sort of medley, the kind that Mike—one of The Grill's servers and bartenders and a recent friend of Scott's—disliked for their banality and lack of attempt to use anything even mildly reminiscent of music that was good or worthwhile or in any way added value to the world, pulsated from the speakers above and around them, lent by the expertly hidden subwoofers a stentorian resonance that such music simply did not deserve. Mike laughed. "You're both drunk," he said. It was Friday night. Or maybe Saturday morning.

"I am not." Kara said. "I'm *not.*"

Mike laughed again. "Oh, yes, you are," he replied, inclining his head. "You're just not as drunk as him." He rolled his eyes in Scott's direction, and Scott's lip was bleeding because he'd tried to take another sip of water.

"Ohmygod you hurt yourself," Kara said, turning to Scott, bumping her elbow on the table. They were sitting at a table in the corner, Scott and Mike on one side, Kara on the other. Angie had been sitting there too, but she'd wandered off to places unknown. The room was dimly lit.

"I'm fine," Scott said, inhaling sharply, sort of a hiss, as he bumped the glass into his lip again. "I'm okay."

Mike grinned. He took a long sip of his Diet Coke.

During the day and early evening, O'Darren's Family Pub was just that: a low-key if not popular locally owned restaurant and bar with good food and a selection of draft beers that, while nothing fancy, was respectable, featuring, along with your standard domestics like Bud Light, Miller Genuine Draft, and Coors Light, some tastier choices, including Guinness, Killians, Yeungling (both Lager and Black and Tan), and the seasonal selections from Great Lakes and Rustbelt, a local beer brewed in an old Youngstown train station. O'Darren's advertised itself as a casual affair, catering to families and middle-aged couples who enjoyed a quiet, warm, friendly environment. The reuben, which was served on marble rye and made with homemade sauerkraut, was particularly popular.

After 10:00 PM on weekends, though, O'Darren's became an almost different establishment entirely. The music was turned up significantly louder. The families and middle-aged couples went home and were replaced with college students and different, younger middle-aged couples and with high school students who had managed to get their hands on passable fake IDs. A brawny man with short-cropped white hair and a goatee and beefy arms bulging underneath a tight black or white or grey t-shirt stood just outside the doorway checking IDs and cracking jokes with regulars and staring down barely pubescent high school students whose fake IDs were laughable or nonexistent. The dress code was relaxed, and midriffs were exposed and cleavage flaunted both by employees and customers. The main lights were dimmed and the secondary lights were set to a violent, epileptic pulsing rhythm. Draft prices were cut in half. Bud Light bottles were only a dollar. Shots were three-fifty or two for six bucks. Shots were downed two at a time. Profanities peppered conversations. Hips gyrated and grinded with the rhythm of the music. Sometimes punches were thrown and more punches were thrown and arms were held back and brawlers were ejected from the building. Tongues found their ways into unfamiliar mouths. Drinks were spilled. Laughs were shared. Men and women enjoyed themselves raucously.

The carbonation burned down Mike's throat, pleasant in that painful way.

Mike The Bartender didn't drink alcohol. He smoked marijuana sometimes, though, usually when meditating— nothing opens up the mind like breathing meditation and just a hit or two of some quality weed, he always said. He smoked cigarettes too, but not often, not packs a day like some people he knew, and he was thinking about quitting, actually. He didn't drink, though, and he hadn't had any alcohol in years. He used to drink as much as anybody, and he favored good whiskey and cheap beer, but his father had died six years ago of liver failure caused by decades of alcoholism and bodily abuse, and Mike watched his father die and watched his mother watch his father die, and he knew that he didn't want to be that person that his father was, and so that was it for him and alcohol, and he went on to get his bartending license at a class the university taught one summer for six hundred bucks without ever taking a sip, and he started working at The Grill three years ago only to learn that casual dining restaurants hardly require their bartenders to know anything about mixing drinks at all.

So Mike drank Diet Coke almost exclusively, and sometimes he drank Arnold Palmers.

Scott had moved to the other side of the booth, next to Kara. She had her head turned toward his, her finger on his bleeding lip.

Mike The Bartender was a Zen Buddhist. He wasn't born a Zen Buddhist, of course—he wasn't born anything, a truth he realized in his preteens while at church with his parents one Sunday listening to Father Johnson drivel on about the importance of raising "good Catholic children, good God-fearing Catholic children." Even as Father Johnson had said it, Mike began to feel not entirely comfortable with the statement. During the drive home from Mass that day, Mike posited a question: "Dad," he said. "Dad, what really are Catholic children?"

"Hmmm? 'S that?" Mike's father was driving the car, and he looked up into the rearview mirror, making eye contact that wasn't actually eye contact but more like reflected eye contact. It should be noted that his dad wasn't drunk, not yet; he may have had a serious drinking problem, but he never broke the law, never drank and drove, and he would never go to church with alcohol in his system, wouldn't dream of it—church, after all, was for worshipping, not drinking, except, of course, for communion, but that was something different. And besides, his dad never drank before noon anyway, never, so getting drunk before Sunday Mass just wouldn't happen.

"What makes a child a Catholic child?" Mike asked again. He saw, through the mirror, his father's eyes drift off to the right and his head turn slightly in the same direction. Mike knew that look, even if he could see only half of it. It was the look his father gave his mother whenever Mike brought up a topic that they weren't sure how to talk about. Mike saw the look a lot, and he knew that his mother, even though he couldn't see her from his spot in the back seat of the family Oldsmobile, was giving his father the exact same look right back.

"Well," his mother said as his father turned his eyes back toward the road, "well, how exactly do you mean?"

"I mean it how I said it, I guess," Mike said. "Father Johnson said to raise 'good Catholic children' "—Mike made quotes in the air with his fingers, quotes which benefited only himself really, since neither of his parents were making eye contact with him now or looking at him in the back seat in any way—"and that just seems maybe disingenuous to me, is all."

His father raised an eyebrow. Mike saw it through the mirror. "Disingenuous."

"I just don't see how children can be Catholic," Mike went on. "I don't really see how children can be anything, since they don't exactly know what any of that really means, I mean like *really* means, you know? So it's just like, well. Because Father Johnson said,"—air quotes again—" 'we must raise good Catholic children,' and I guess all I'm saying is that, actually, parents would be raising good Catholic adults, because the children, when they're children, can't decide what religion they want to be."

Mike's mother had groaned quietly. "Then how do you explain you?"

"I'm not a child." Mike said this like he would state any fact.

"You're a child."

"Then I'm not Catholic."

The car pulled up to a red light, and Mike's father turned his head around. "How's that now?"

"I'm not saying that I don't want to be Catholic or anything, but," Mike shrugged, "maybe I don't."

"Ha, I'm afraid it's too late for that, kiddo. You were baptized when you were a week old. You're definitely Catholic."

The light turned green.

"Jesus wasn't Catholic."

The car swerved slightly to left.

"Oh ho ho," Mike's mother was laughing. Actually laughing. "You need to pay more attention in church, Mikey. Jesus was baptized. Trust me, he was Catholic."

Mike didn't continue on with the conversation, but when he got home that day, he picked up his Bible for the first time, and within the next two years had read it cover-to-cover twice. By the time he was fourteen, he knew that he most certainly didn't believe in any brand of Christianity anymore. He didn't tell anyone, not right away, but he was pretty sure he was an atheist, and really, he supposed he always had been. He'd definitely been born an atheist—the way he saw it, all children were born atheists—and despite the efforts of others—parents, teachers, church figures—to convince him otherwise, a process that, admittedly, ended up working on most children, he just never got around to believing in a god, at least not the way most people seemed to believe in a god. Then, during his freshman year of high school while he was researching a social studies report that he'd decided to base on the topic of world religions, Mike became intensely fascinated with Buddhism. It struck him, much to his surprise, as, if not right, then at the very least a sensible way to live, perhaps even more Christian than Christianity with regard to decent human values and morals. Buddhism wasn't exactly atheistic, Mike noted, and it was certainly spiritual, but it was spiritual without letting spirituality get in the way of living. It was, Mike decided, *nontheistic* more than anything, and he liked that. He'd also discovered marijuana by this point, and he found Buddhist philosophy to be compatibly mellow.

When he told his parents that he no longer wished to be Catholic, and that in fact he hadn't considered himself one for some time, and that he was now a Buddhist, their response was far less aggressive than he'd expected. "You can't be a Buddhist," his mom said. "You were baptized as a Catholic when you were a baby. You can't exactly get re-baptized as a Buddhist, now can you?"

"You don't get baptized as a Buddhist, Mom," Mike said. "You just decide that you want to be one and then that's it. Put simply, anyway."

His mom was mildly incredulous. "If you aren't baptized as a Buddhist, then I don't see how you can be one."

"And besides," Mike's father said, opening the refrigerator and taking out his third cold beer so far that evening, "what about God?" He said it as if that was all there was to it. Just God. You know, but what about God?

"Have you ever read the Bible?" Mike said. "God's kind of an asshole."

His parents didn't say anything more about his conversion after that, and he suspected they didn't really care all that much about it. They hadn't been to church much in the last couple years, anyway.

By the time he was twenty, Mike had saved up a decent amount of money, and he planned on traveling to the East for a while to further his study and his practice, but that's when his father's health began to take a turn for the worse, and so Mike decided to stay home for a while and support his mother since his father couldn't really work anymore. Six months later, Mike started smoking cigarettes in addition to the weed. And a year after that, almost seven years ago now, Mike's father's liver failed and he died.

Angela sauntered over to the table, a fresh Long Island Iced Tea in her hand. "Oh dear God," she said, setting the drink down at the edge of the table and staring. "What are you two getting yourselves up to?"

Mike slid over against the wall of the booth, making room next to him for Angela. "They're drunk."

"Hey!" Scott said, turning his head towards them and holding up an index finger. And then, lowering his voice almost to a whisper: "I resent the implication that I'm drunk."

"Who's implying? You're drunk."

Scott smirked and turned back to Kara, whose finger found its way inside his mouth. "You're still bleeding," she said.

"Oh." Angela frowned, noticing the lip for the first time. "He *is* bleeding. What happened?"

Mike smiled behind his glass as he took another sip. "He's drunk."

Angela raised her eyebrows in an expression of acute understanding and acceptance and nodded. "Careful, you two. You drink too much and you'll both turn into me. Or Kara will end up with another kid."

Kara's daughter was with her father this weekend—Kara's daughter's father, not Kara's father, who (Kara's father) had died a long time ago. If Kara could have had it her way, her daughter would never see that fucker again, but until she could convince the courts otherwise, they insisted that Derek Aasole had a legal right to see his daughter at least every other weekend. Oh and how Kara hated that her daughter shared that fucker's last name, and what had she been thinking when Derek had given the name to the nurse and she'd watched the nurse write it down: Eleanor Katerina Aasole? What the hell kind of terrible mother lets a man name a baby Eleanor? And then of course the fact that Derek's last name was Aasole—and that really was his last name—had hit her with the force of some sort of hilarious nuclear bomb when she saw it on her daughter's birth certificate, and, drugged as she was, she couldn't help but giggle at the time—the asshole's name actually sounded like "asshole" and how the fuck hadn't she noticed it before? How hadn't she made the connection when she met him the year before? Maybe it was that suit he'd been wearing and the way it seemed to clean him up, even if it was too large and the shirt and tie an obnoxious combination of black and gold, and yet still, despite its sloppiness and cheapness and worldliness, the suit had somehow detracted from the redness of his eyes, and the heavy cloud of cologne surrounding him had masked the smells of tobacco and crack cocaine that permeated his skin and hair enough that she felt comfortable choosing to ignore them. And somehow, weeks later, even as they were naked and he was fucking her and impregnating her, her eyes still didn't see the track marks on his arms, and of course she knew—we always know, she told herself even now—but her youth and her lust and her orgasms and her perceived shitty childhood were exactly the sort of blinders she was willing to put on when she was twenty years old, so she wore them with the innocence of the not-so-innocent and pretended that everything was okay and that she had the best man in the world and oh how she'd been kidding herself even as she knew she was kidding herself. The asshole's name was Aasole, for fuck's sake.

But maybe he had changed now, just like he said he would. He'd spent that month in rehab, and he said he was clean and sober—maybe she should believe him and forgive him. He lived in Toledo now and held a steady construction job and promised that he wanted to take care of Kara and Ellie, if only Kara would let him prove it. Besides, Ellie loved her daddy; Kara couldn't deny her baby girl that. And though she might have hated herself for it, Kara loved him too. She prayed to Jesus about the situation every day.

Of course, none of this would stop her from going home with Scott tonight. She was drunk and feeling pretty good, and besides, her fingers were already in his mouth, so in both their minds sex seemed like the next logical step. Mike offered to drive them both home since he was completely sober, but they declined. Scott lived only a couple blocks from O'Darren's, which in turn was only a couple blocks from The Grill, so Kara would walk with him and just stay the night. It's what Scott would have done anyway since he still didn't own a car right now. Kara would leave her car in the lot and Scott would walk her back to get it tomorrow.

Mike and Angela exchanged a glance, both a little uncomfortable with the fact that they knew their coworkers were almost definitely going to sleep with each other, but they also acknowledged that Scott and Kara were both adults, so whatever.

"Okay, just be careful, is all," Mike said as Scott and Kara both stood from the table. "You guys work tomorrow?"

"Tomorrow night," Scott said.

Kara shook her head. "Nah, I'm off tomorrow. Sunday morning, though?"

Mike smiled. "Sure. Sure. See you Sunday morning." They all worked most Sunday mornings. Geoff was particularly paranoid about Sundays, on which The Grill opened early and served brunch in addition to the regular menu, and on which one never knew how busy or how slow things were going to get, so he usually scheduled a full front-of-the-house staff.

Scott and Kara wandered out the door, leaving their empty glasses behind on the table. Mike turned to Angela, who was nursing her Long Island. "And so then, what about you? You work at all the rest of the weekend?"

Angela nodded. "Yup. I always work the weekends." She held her drink up in front of her face. The strobing light shined through the dark liquid. She sighed. "Isn't that right, Mr. Long Island? *Yes it is.*"

The day had been warm, but the night was noticeably cooler as Scott and Kara stepped out into it. Summer was coming to an abrupt close in Youngstown and the leaves would start changing any week now. The onset of fall filled Scott with anticipation.

Every time the seasons changed from one into the next—from autumn to winter, from winter to spring, from spring to summer, and as now, from summer back to autumn—Scott held a secret hope that the transition would bring something new for him as well. Sometimes it even did—a new struggle, a new relationship, a new loss, a new job at a new restaurant—but rarely was the change the kind he wanted.

Kara had her left arm looped inside Scott's right as they walked. She held her arm across her torso, her hand on her left elbow so that she was close to him, pressed up against his body. Scott wasn't especially tall, but Kara wasn't tall at all, so when she tried to lay her head on his shoulder, it rested on the side, on the muscle. Kara's gait was a little unsteady, but she was capable of a straight line, and Scott helped her along. The fresh night air was sobering him up; then again, maybe he hadn't been all that drunk in the first place but instead was just enjoying the excuse to act intoxicated, to say and do things, silly things, that he felt like saying and doing but otherwise would never, to make a fool of himself, essentially.

In the darkness, this part of the city was peaceful. Youngstown wasn't a big city, but it wasn't exactly small, either. It had its bad neighborhoods and its dangerous neighborhoods, and most of the buildings and houses were nearly a hundred years old and many of them were older, but there was a lot to do here and a lot to love, if one wanted to look. There was the university and the park and the Butler Museum of American Art. The recent reconstructionist movement had done much to revitalize the once dying city as well. Dubbed "Youngstown 2010," the plan was instated in 2002 as a detailed vision to reinvent a city that had been shrinking since the steel mills shut down in the 70s and 80s. Admittedly, the idea had fizzled out a couple of years earlier than its name might suggest, but a great deal of good had come from it: There was the convocation center, which was originally called the Chevy Center when it opened, with the naming rights belonging to General Motors (who was responsible for most of the economic growth in the city), and which was now called the Covelli Center after Sam Covelli, who owned a good deal of the area's franchise restaurants (not The Grill, which is strictly corporate-owned in all but its Hawaii locations), acquired the naming rights in 2009. With the center came many high-profile concerts—the kinds one would usually have to travel to Pittsburgh or Cleveland to see, artists like Elton John and Bob Dylan and Nickelback and Weird Al Yankovic—and even, briefly, Youngstown's very own professional hockey team. Several new apartment buildings had been erected under the 2010 plan, and the years between 2002 and 2008 saw a boon in the number of new nightclubs, restaurants, and bars opening in the city, most of which, granted, had closed not long after, but some, including O'Darren's, were still lucky enough to be experiencing strong business.

Scott had spent most of his life in the suburbs just outside this city, and as much as he hated it here, he liked it here.

His apartment was only two blocks from the bar, and it took Scott and Kara all of ten minutes to arrive at the building, even walking as slow as they were. Scott lived in one of the newer buildings, one of the products of Youngstown 2010. They rode the elevator to the third floor—Scott didn't know how Kara or he would do with stairs right now and decided not to risk it—and Scott untangled his arm from hers and fished in his pocket for his key.

"It's nice," Kara said, as they stepped through the doorway.

"It's affordable," Scott said.

The apartment was small but not untidy, and even though Scott had little in the way of furniture, it was still cramped. There was a sofa and a folding chair and a small wooden coffee table. On the table was a laptop computer and a paperback novel by Tom Clancy. A collection of free weights and even a kettlebell sat on the floor near the wall, under the window, and a shelf next to the window was filled with more paperbacks and a few workout DVDs.

The kitchen, while also small, was clean. A bowl of fruit—apples and bananas and two oranges and a mango—sat on the counter between the kitchen and the living room. There was no dining room or dining room table, but there were two stools under the counter. A metal coffeepot sat next to the sink. Despite its size, everything about the apartment was modern and clean.

"It really is nice," Kara said. "I mean it."

"Thanks."

"Mmmhmm."

"Well—"

"Can I use your bathroom?" Kara said.

"Oh, yeah, of course. Here. It's right here." Scott led her down a short hallway just off the living room with two doors at the end. He pointed to one. "That's the bathroom."

"Then that's your bedroom, I take it," Kara said, gesturing to the other door, which was open.

"Yeah."

"Okay, cool. I'll be right out."

Scott nodded.

Scott was still wearing his black t-shirt and black pants from work—he hadn't had a chance to change before heading over to O'Darren's—and he was aware of the fact that he smelled of food. He walked into the bedroom, which contained only a queen-sized bed, a nightstand, and a small closet. He took his cell phone from his pocket (his cellular service had almost been cancelled by the provider last month due to lack of payment, but he'd managed to square that away after getting the job) and plugged it into its charger on the nightstand. Next to it he set his wallet and his keys. There were condoms in the drawer. He opened the closet and took off his shirt, draping it over the side of the hamper carefully. Then he did the same with his pants. He considered changing his boxers for a second before deciding that he should, but before he could finish pulling the new pair on, Kara came into the room.

"So, how are you liking The Gr— Oh. Shit. Sorry."

Scott pivoted, hopping on one foot, the other one in the leg of the boxers. He stood up straight when he saw her, dropping the shorts to the floor. "It's okay," he said, unfazed. He stepped his second foot into the boxers and knelt down and pulled them up.

"You're pretty comfortable with yourself, aren't you?" Kara observed. "With your body, I mean."

Scott shrugged. "I didn't used to be."

Kara pulled her top off, revealing a black bra and a slim, tight stomach. "I wish I could be like that," she said, "but having a baby kind of messes that whole body image thing up for you."

"Yeah, well," Scott said again. "I think you look great."

They both just stood there for several seconds. The moment wasn't awkward, just there. And then Kara walked over to the bed and pulled the covers down and climbed under them. Scott climbed in next to her. "You know," she said. "I'm not really feeling all that drunk anymore."

"Yeah, me either."

"So, how *are* you liking The Grill?"

They both rolled over so they could look at each other. "It's alright," Scott said. "It's pretty much the same as all the other restaurants I've worked at. Geoff's an idiot."

Kara nodded. "So's R.J., but R.J.'s more of a lovable idiot. You get used to him. Geoff, not so much."

"But everyone else is pretty great," Scott said, smiling. "You, Mike, Angie, Lori—I enjoy working with all of you."

"Me too. I think Lori really likes you, by the way."

"You think so? She's cute."

"She's a sweetheart," Kara said, "but she's young."

"We're all young." Scott said.

"You know what I mean. She's innocent and everything. I mean, she's not like a virgin or anything—I know this for sure—we talk a lot and hang out a lot—but she's also super happy and religious and everything. I think she thinks she wants to experience certain things, but then at the same time doesn't."

"I know what you mean. She's quite flirtatious."

"Yes, she is." And Kara laughed as if remembering. "You should try flirting back with her though. Like really flirting with her. She doesn't always know how to respond when someone flirts back. It's funny."

Scott and Kara both rolled onto their backs, staring up at the ceiling. They lay like that for several minutes, silent, breathing, the light still on on the nightstand next to Scott. They smelled of food and sweat and alcohol.

"So," Scott said.

"So."

"Do you . . . want to . . ."

"Actually," Kara said, "I kind of want a shower, you know?"

Scott nodded. "Yeah. Okay."

"I mean, I'm sure you want one too. It's been a long day."

"I'm okay."

"Yes. Well." Kara slid out from under the covers and stood.

"There's a clean towel in the little closet next to the sink," Scott said.

Scott's mind was buzzing, but it was just a dull buzz now, an exhausted pressure tugging at the edges of his brain.

"You could, you know, shower *with* me."

Scott stared at the ceiling, imagining a fan there, imagining it spinning clockwise and wobbling precariously as it spun. His lip hurt and his head was cloudy. "Yeah. Okay."

Seven Months Pre Brand-Changing Day, 2012

Geoff McCree was running around like a head with its chicken cut off or some such. It was Sunday and the lunch shift. Most weeks, Sunday lunch shift was a very busy period for The Grill, but on this particular Sunday the shift was running smoothly and nobody save for Geoff seemed to be having any problems doing their job.

"I need runners! Runners and help runners!"

Scott, who had been running a trayful of dirty dishes to the dish station, where Eddie, the dishwasher, methodically moved dish from counter to tank and from tank to drying rack while humming along with a distinctly Latino dance tune blasting from a pair of plastic headphones, turned and scuttled quickly out of the kitchen before Geoff took note of his presence, which it wasn't likely that he would, but nevertheless. He found outside the swinging door Mike, who was on his phone, typing a text message, which you weren't supposed to do in the dining room but which everyone did anyway. "The hell is he on about?" Mike said.

"Oh, you know," Scott said. "There's, what, like three orders just came up out of the window, maybe like nine or ten plates, and all the servers whose orders they are are back there ready to pick them up just fine, don't even need a follow."

Mike tucked his phone into the pocket of his apron and

walked over to the bar—he was serving today, not bartending, because Angela was bartending, but he had rung in several mixed fruit teas a few moments earlier—and Scott followed him. "He's stressing everybody out."

"Yeah, or at least most of us. I'm good."

"Hey, I'm good, too. I have like three tables and two of them have their food, and I'm just getting drinks for the other one. I haven't had more than five tables all day."

Angela was universally regarded as one of the most physically attractive employees at The Grill, and though she wasn't the most intelligent and had a bizarre penchant for talking to inanimate objects as if they were sentient, thinking beings who might respond, she was a good bartender and had been working at The Grill for something like five years. She had Mike's fruit teas, one strawberry and two passion fruit, up in the bar window by the time he approached.

"These mine?" Mike asked.

"Yes sir," Angela said, her voice sort of *cutesy*. And she turned around to continue her conversation with a regular bar guest, who Scott had seen in the restaurant often at about this time, and who usually managed to get himself inebriated on white wine by three in the afternoon most days.

Mike trayed the drinks and extended his arm through the bar window to grab three plastic-covered straws, but then he changed his mind and grabbed the paper-covered ones instead, because the paper-covered ones were bigger, diametrically, and so it was easier to suck the chunks of fruit in the fruit teas through them. "Tips have only been so-so, though, but that's the trade-off."

"Same here. Hey, so where's R.J. anyway? He usually runs shift on Sunday."

"Vacation. Hunting or something."

"He hunts a lot."

There was a soft thud as Lori opened one of the deadly swinging kitchen doors that on the outside had a sign marked "NO" with her shoulder because each hand held a hot plate of food and the door had slammed into the wall.

Mike, before walking off towards his table with the fruit teas, nodded at Lori as she passed and said, "How's that going?"

Scott smiled. "Really well," he said.

There'd been this bonfire about three weeks ago over on the shore of Lake Milton. Mike had arranged the thing. He arranged bonfires often; usually, he had them at his house, where he had built a serviceable fire pit in the back yard, but this one he'd decided to have on the lake since summer was coming to its inevitable end (summer always ends) and the last warm days of the year would soon be behind them all. At the bonfire, Scott spent most of the night talking to Lori, who had recently broken up with her boyfriend of three years. There was alcohol, but she didn't drink it and so neither did he. Their banter quickly turned to deeper conversation, and Scott was immediately that evening more taken with the idea of Lori than he had been with anyone: her smile, her laughter, her wit, the way the sunlight reflected off her golden hair, damp from a dip in the lake, and off the sand that covered her long legs. They went to the movies only two days later, alone, and then for coffee at a nearby Starbucks. He had dinner at her parents' house the very next weekend—roast beef that fell apart like magic and potatoes and roasted baby carrots—where she introduced him to the wonders of Dr. Who on DVD, and they'd watched the entire first season that evening and that night and into the following morning. In the time since then, they'd been seeing more and more of each other, and Scott had begun to want to enjoy it here.

"I need runners! Runners and help runners! Lots of runners!"

Brand-Changing Day, 2012

Geoff McCree was cursing noncommittally as he pulled his Chrysler Sebring into The Grill's empty parking lot.

"Dammit. Dammit dammit dammit."

He'd debated with himself, of course, about whether or not he should wait until he got to the restaurant before he opened the wrapping around the breakfast sandwich. He'd ordered bacon this morning instead of sausage, which was unusual just because he almost always ordered sausage, and when he didn't order sausage he ordered Canadian bacon, not the crispy, salty bacon strips he'd ordered today, but whatever—he really didn't care what kind of meat he was eating or how processed it was; he was hungry. He ended up opening the sandwich about two miles away from the restaurant, because he just couldn't help himself, and even as he went to take his first bite, balancing the greasy bag on his knee instead of setting it on the seat next him, a nice big hot glob (he could think of no better word than glob; in fact, "glob" was a large part of Geoff's working vocabulary) of hydrogenated vegetable oil (Geoff, though, didn't know or care what kind of oil it was) rolled out of a tiny opening in the folds of the bottom of the paper and hung there, high above Geoff's white shirt, waiting, dangling.

When Geoff's teeth sunk into the croissant and the

scrambled egg and the bacon and processed American Cheese Product from Kraft and a small bit of paper that he hadn't quite pulled out of the way, the glob of grease was pushed, literally pushed, from its stalactitical position at the bottom of the wrapping by another glob of grease expunged from the sandwich by the force of Geoff's initial ravenous chomp, and it fell onto Geoff's fingers and then split off into two separate streams of oil, one burning its way down Geoff's arm and the other dripping onto his white t-shirt, staining the shirt in an instant and causing Geoff to wince and grunt at the pain of the grease on his skin. He had his jacket on, but it was open and the grease didn't touch it. And as it turned out, the sandwich itself was too hot for Geoff's tongue, having been wrapped in paper and popped in a microwave and nuked so that it got hot and so that the paper sealed that heat in the sandwich and in itself, so when Geoff bit into it, at the same time that the oil burned his skin and dirtied his clothes, the meat and the cheese scalded the inside of his mouth; he'd avoided yet sipping on his coffee for fear of it scalding his mouth in the same way.

"Dammit. Dammit dammit dammit."

And now his steering wheel was greasy, too. He suddenly felt like he hadn't showered today, even though he had. And of course it was brand-changing day and he'd be at the restaurant all day overseeing the roll-out of the new menu items and the new policies and procedures, and now he'd feel gross the entire time. It wasn't like he'd been planning to wear the white t-shirt the entire day—or, more accurately, he had, it's just that he was going to wear it under the striped dress shirt and with the dress pants that he would put on before the store opened was all—but the feeling of grease on one's face and arms does not go away with just a change of clothes, and in fact, Geoff sort of thought as he looked down at the stain on the part of his shirt that covered his belly, which had visible rolls when he was sitting like this, it really doesn't go away at all.

He put the car in park and turned off the ignition. He rewrapped the sandwich and placed it in the bag. They hadn't put any napkins in the bag, but he had some in the glove compartment, accumulated from past visits to various fast food chains. He pulled a wad of them out and wiped his face and the underside of his forearm and the steering wheel and tossed the wad onto the floor of the car. Grunting again, he unplugged the iPhone from the aux-jack and, phone in one hand and Dunkin' Donuts bag and hot medium coffee with cream and two sugars in the other, first three fingers and thumb around the cup and the bag clenched precariously in between his palm and his pinky, exited the vehicle.

The restaurant was empty and quiet, and Geoff sat in the office and finished his breakfast in greasy peace before grabbing his clipboard and heading into the coolers. Most mornings, he was as apathetic to pulls and counts as he was towards everything —they had to be done, and he did them—but this morning, he was almost looking forward to being cold and alone, comfortable in his solitude and his aloneness.

He made check marks on the clipboard as he walked among the shelves and boxes of food. They were still missing the cartons of cream for the new cream procedure: before, servers would always bring two creamers per cup every time a customer ordered coffee, and the creamers were in those little plastic single-serving things that you pull the top off of before pouring, but starting today the procedure would be to ask first if the customer wanted cream with his coffee or her coffee, and if the customer said "Yes, please!" or "What the hell kind of question is that? Of course I want cream with my damn coffee!" the server would pour the cream—actually, half-n-half—from a carton and into one of these cute little silver pitchers, and if the customer didn't want cream, well then, no cream. The goal of the whole thing was to present a classier image to the customer than before and also to save money. The little silver pitchers, hundreds of them, had arrived last week, but for some reason the cream itself didn't come with yesterday's shipment like it was supposed to. They still had a box of the old creamers on the shelf, not yet expired, so the servers could just empty those into the little silver pitchers for now. The restaurant wasn't missing anything else, so that was good.

Geoff's apathy extended to most things: his wife, his unborn child, the idea of being a father at 42 (43 if his wife didn't have her baby in the next three weeks, which she probably would because she was already eight-and-a-half months along), doing pulls and counts in the coolers and the stockroom early in the morning before the restaurant opened, his employees and their desires and concerns, wine and cheese and the temperature of his steak (although he did prefer it well-done, he'd eat it however it was presented to him) and food in general (unless the food was served in his restaurant and a customer was complaining about it, in which case he became immediately concerned and engrossed in finding and addressing the issue), sports (except for football, and even then he only really cared about the Pittsburgh Steelers, and even that only came from having been raised by a father who was obsessed with the team), movies (what his wife referred to as "films"), books, music (and if he was asked what music he wanted to listen to, if given the choice, he'd pick something like Bruce Springsteen or Led Zeppelin or Rod Stewart because it was music that everybody was supposed to like and because it had a safeness about it, like it pretended to have feelings and care about whatever it was about, but really it was, well, safe), God, technology, politics. Most of these things just *were* for him, as in they existed but had no general impact on his thoughts, feelings, or emotions.

He did care about sex, at least sometimes, just not really about sex with his wife. He learned this a couple months ago when he engaged in a brief, mediocre affair with Cathy Blumstein, the general manager of The Grill's Jamestown store. He hadn't meant for it to happen, and he even now considered himself a good husband and faithful human, but it sort of just did. Corporate had just sent out an email about the new brand-changing initiative, but the email had been light on details, odd because typically whenever the company made policy or menu changes like this, it just sent the details along straight away and left the individual general managers to sort things out. Maybe there would be a conference call or two or even a visit from the regional manager just to make sure everybody knew exactly how things were to be carried out, but for the most part it was never a big deal. This time, however, the email announced only that big changes would soon be coming to Earl's American Restaurant Group and regional meetings would be held all around the world in the coming weeks, and that it was all so exciting, and that everybody should be proud to be part of this momentous milestone in the company's history.

In the case of The Grill's Northeast Region, also called Region 23, of which the Youngstown store was a part, the big meeting was held at a Holiday Inn in Erie, PA, and was attended by the GMs of nineteen other stores. It just so happened that Cathy Blumstein ended up sitting next to Geoff in the hotel's medium-sized conference room. Cathy sat on Geoff's left and

George Paternoster from the Akron store sat on his right. Geoff knew George from way back; they'd both been in charge of their respective locations for over fourteen years now and were friends in that way that two people who have the same life and the same general disinterest in most things are friends. They even met up in Pittsburgh together for Steelers games every now and then, and their wives knew each other and talked on the phone sometimes. George was a very round man with a misogynistic laugh and an extreme enthusiasm for his restaurant and misogyny and nothing else, so he was, more than anyone, excited to be at the meeting. When he saw Cathy sit next to Geoff, he nudged him in the ribs and winked. Geoff looked to his left and then back at George and rolled his eyes and shook his head.

"How's it goin', buddy?" George asked him, his voice just one among the several other conversations happening in the conference room, where the meeting had not yet started. He extended his right hand and twisted his bulbous torso.

Geoff shook the hand. "Oh, you know, it's fine."

As they shook, George winked again and said, "And how 'bout you, Cathy? How you doing?"

Cathy Blumstein's attention was clearly unfocused as her eyes searched the room. She seemed to be looking for, but not finding, familiar faces. When she heard George, though, she turned. "Hey, George!" she said. "Hey! It's good to see you."

George looked at Geoff. "Cathy is the new GM over at the Jamestown store. She just finished her training down in Akron with me, what, oh, about a month ago."

"Yes, about that long," Cathy said.

"Yeah, well. So, hey! This here is Geoff. He's from way down in Youngstown."

"Nice to meet you," Cathy said, smiling at Geoff. She was

young, maybe thirty, and her teeth were white. Her hair was dark brown and tied up in a bun at the top of the back of her head. There were lines beginning to form just around her eyes. She wasn't particularly beautiful, but neither was she unattractive.

"Me and Geoff are gonna go out after this shindig's over—get some drinks, try and rustle up a few of the other GMs to join us. You in?"

Geoff frowned. "We are—?" He didn't remember making specific plans.

"Sure," Cathy said, "why not? I don't really know anybody else here, so."

"Great! It'll be a roaring good time."

The regional manager approached the podium at the front of the room then, asking for quiet and thanking everybody for coming. Big exciting things in store for the company. He held a small remote control in his hand, and when he pressed a button the first slide of a poorly designed PowerPoint presentation lit up on the projector screen next to the podium.

"Listen," Geoff whispered to George. "I wasn't planning on staying after or anything. I have a bit of a drive, and I wanted to just start heading home after the meeting."

"You mean you don't have a hotel room here?"

"No."

"Well, then, man, we've got to get you one. You're going to wanna stay the night. Cathy will fuck anyone who even so much as buys her a drink. You gotta get in on that. Trust me, I've taken it for a ride or two, and she'll bang your balls off."

Geoff glanced quickly to his left, but Cathy didn't seem to have heard the comment. "George . . ." Geoff whispered through tight lips and clamped teeth. "What are you talking about? I'm not cheating on my wife, who's pregnant, by the way."

"So what. And when was the last time your wife gave you some, huh? The night you got her pregnant, I bet. Right? Right? Ah, see, I *am* right. I've got kids, too, you forget. This is just a thing we do, guys like us. Our wives don't care about us—they don't understand the responsibility and skill—the *importance*— of running a business the way we do, so we work all day and they get mad—your wife gets mad when you come home late, doesn't she?—and so then they cockblock us. We have a right to fuck a bitch, man."

"That's ridiculous—"

"And anyway, you're probably the only person here who didn't book a hotel room, you know, take the opportunity to get away for a day or two."

"We have stores to run."

"We have assistant managers to run our stores for us. Stick around tonight. Erie's an okay place. Good bars."

Geoff considered, feigning more reluctance than he felt. R.J. was running the shifts today; Geoff supposed he could make him do it tomorrow too, or at least tomorrow morning. Okay, yeah, that could work. Geoff would stay tonight and leave in the morning and arrive in time to supervise the evening shift. "Okay, okay," he whispered. "I'll hang out, I guess. But I'm not cheating on my wife, and you're crazy if you think I am."

It turned out that cheating on his wife was something Geoff was far more willing to do than he'd anticipated. In fact, it was easy. He booked a room at the Holiday Inn like everyone else, but never saw the inside of it. One minute, he was drinking his third Coors Light in this dark, loud place on the lake at a long, wide table with a group of other managers, and the next thing he knew, with no real explanation or excuse for how it had happened, he was in Cathy Blumstein's hotel room with his penis inside her having what to him qualified as decent sex. She kept calling out his name, asking him to do certain things, but they weren't really things he was interested in doing, and so he just kind of humped away like he always did during coitus (another one of those words he would never have used). And when it was over a few minutes later, he fell asleep in her bed while she went downstairs to the hotel bar. He thought he might have remembered seeing her again in the room in the early morning, but he was tired and unsure.

After the deed was done and the night was over and the morning had come, Geoff had no feelings about what he'd done. His wife didn't have to know, and he had no compulsion to tell her or anybody else. He drove home to Youngstown in his Sebring, excited about the upcoming brand-changing, and by the time he arrived at the restaurant, the sex act of the night before was hardly a blip on his memory. He'd only thought about it a small handful of times between then and now, and even then he never dwelled on it. His wife was having a baby, and it was his baby and she was his wife, so anything that happened outside of that arrangement didn't mean anything to anyone, least of all him. What happened inside of that arrangement hardly mattered either.

The restaurant mattered. Brand-changing day mattered.

Geoff finished the counts just before 9:30 AM. He tucked the clipboard under his arm and pulled a box from a shelf in the dry-storage room. It was a heavy box, but he balanced it on his shoulder and managed to carry it to the server line, dropping it on the counter violently, wincing. Using a steak knife to cut the tape, he opened the box and tipped it over. A dozen large aprons, each one individually wrapped, spilled out onto the metal countertop. The aprons the servers had been wearing until today were plain, black pieces of fabric, but these ones on the counter matched The Grill's new striped motif, a pattern shared by the new signage on the front of the restaurant and the new button-down, collared shirts that the male bartenders were now required to wear. Geoff liked the new uniforms. He liked them a lot.

Geoff's coffee was still in the office next to the computer, but it was cold now, and so Geoff poured a bag of coffee into the kitchen's industrial coffee maker (a Bunn 23001.0000 Airport Coffee Maker Pourover) and turned it on and pressed BREW. Geoff thought it made good coffee.

As he waited for the pot of coffee to brew, which doesn't take long with these industrial coffee makers, he walked back into the office and sat in the chair.

There is an eeriness that comes with being alone in an American chain restaurant. The place was silent and empty and cold, especially cold early in the morning before bodies had begun to move the air around. The only sounds were the hum of the fluorescent lights in the back of the house—the front of the house lights always stayed off until fifteen minutes before the place opened for lunch—and the buzz of coolant moving through pipes and tubes in the walk-ins and uprights. There was the occasional *pop* as pressure was released in the CO_2 cartridges of the beer and soda taps. And of course today there was also the mechanical *whir* of the industrial coffee maker and the *drip drip drip* as freshly burnt coffee poured into the large metal pot, which, starting today, as one of the new brand guidelines, all employees are to refer to, along with pitchers, as "carafes."

Geoff thought about turning on some music, stood to reach

the audio system's dial, but he heard footsteps moving through the kitchen, and then an old man was in the office doorway.

"Morning, Geoff," the man said.

"Oh, hey there, Michael," Geoff said. "Good morning."

This wasn't the bartender Mike, but rather Michael, the manager-in-training Michael. Michael had been training at The Grill's Youngstown location for almost three months. At 67 years old, he was the oldest general manager-in-training Geoff had ever heard of, but he was energetic and followed directions good, Geoff thought, and he'd probably be a good general manager wherever they assigned him after his training, which was almost over.

"Everything all set for the big day?" Michael asked.

"As ready as I'll ever be," Geoff said, which wasn't exactly an answer to the question Michael had asked, but Geoff didn't realize this.

"Who's all coming in, then?"

Geoff sat back down in the chair and spun toward the computer. He clicked on an icon and a spreadsheet with the week's schedule filled the screen. Geoff highlighted today, Tuesday. "As far as managers, it's just you and me this morning, but R.J. will be in at two to take over for the afternoon, and you and I should both be able to head home, I think. We've got five servers in the morning: Michelle, Betty, and Josh, and Scott and Kara, who are both closing lunch and working doubles, so they'll be here tonight, too. And then we've got eight servers tonight, including Scott and Kara. It's still just a Tuesday, but it *is* a new menu and everything, so I put on a few extra servers than usual because we'll probably get some extra business, what with the coupons that went out at the beginning of the week and everything. Oh, and Mike's on the bar all day, but he won't be in until one because his mom's sick or . . . whatever, so if anyone orders drinks at lunch Josh will have to make them or something."

Michael nodded. "Couldn't we just pull Josh off the floor and put him behind the bar, since he's extra anyway?"

Geoff shook his head. "If we really needed to, we could, but I don't want to do that. Who knows how busy it will get for lunch with all those coupons."

Michael nodded. At The Grill, unlike most other American chain restaurants, bartenders weren't allowed tables of their own, even though there were tables in the bar area that they could easily serve while still making drinks and waiting on bar guests.

"I've got an idea, then," Michael said, pointing to the floor chart, which showed that Josh would be serving the section in the back left corner of the restaurant. "Why don't we just take Josh and move him to this section over here by the bar, in the bar area, that way he's close to the bar in case we do get bar guests."

Geoff stared at the chart, at first unsure what Michael meant, but then he saw it. That *would* make things easier. "Okay," he said, making the adjustments to the chart, which he then printed out before remembering that he didn't need to print the chart out anymore because the hostess stand was computerized now.

"Did you do the counts already?" Michael asked.

"Yes."

"Well, okay, then. I'm going start getting things ready for the servers, then, lend them a hand before they get here."

Geoff stood up. "No, that's not necessary. I have the openers coming in fifteen minutes early today to get everything set up.

They can do it. And the cooks will be in any minute to get things set up behind the line."

Michael nodded. "What, um, do you need me to do, then?"

Six Months Pre Brand-Changing Day, 2012

As they began to spend time alone together, the flirting between Scott and Lori became less overt and more subtle, more natural and less about all the dirty things Scott would do to Lori or Lori would do to Scott, and it became clear to Scott that for Lori, talk had only been talk, and she wasn't prepared to do any of those things.

There was a tree outside Scott's small apartment's small living room's window. It was a tall, broadly branching oak tree, and its leaves were changing quickly these last few days as summer became autumn. It had been one of the last trees to change, a holdout, waiting for the last minute to do its natural thing and die for just a little while. Scott's attention shifted to the tree for a few moments every now and then as he and Lori sat on the couch in his apartment, Scott's back inclined against the armrest, Lori on his lap, her back against his chest, and Scott's white laptop resting on her soft, flat belly. They were already finishing the second series of *Doctor Who*, had just finished "Doomsday," a poignant story about love and loss and multiple dimensions.

When the episode was over, and Scott had to admit it left him feeling a certain emptiness inside, a heartsick, just as Lori had warned him it would, he took the laptop and closed it and placed it gently on the table. And then he wrapped his arms around Lori warmly.

She turned around and he slid down from the armrest so that he was laying on his back on the couch and she was laying on top of him, her face to his. And then her mouth was on his and she was kissing him, and he was kissing her, their tongues warm and wet and soft inside each other's mouths. Scott could smell her hair, her peach shampoo. He'd always had this thing about peach shampoo, this thing where it smelled so real he couldn't fight the desire to taste it, but when he did taste it it was bitter, just shampoo. His hand slid from Lori's shoulders down to her back, and from her back he moved them around and to her belly, feeling the short, soft blonde hairs around her belly button. She had one hand in his hair and the other on his arm, and when she shifted, her knee brushed lightly against his erection. She paused.

"Scott," she said, "I— I don't want to have sex right now."

Scott paused too, and he looked at her. "Okay," he said.

"I'm not a virgin," Lori said. "At all, but . . . and well I don't want to wait until marriage or anything either or anything like that, but I do, you know, want to wait . . . a little while that is. I dated my last boyfriend for a long time, and I need to just go slow right now. At least a little."

Scott said again, breathily, "Okay."

And so they spent the next few hours, and ultimately, the next few months, exploring each other's bodies, but only so far: lips and tongues and necks and ears and breasts and backs and bellies. And Scott told himself every time he was with her that this was the perfection he'd been striving for his entire life—this sort of relationship with this sort of person. That there were things about Lori that made it so different than every other time before: her youth (even though she was only slightly younger than him, she possessed an innocence he wished he could reclaim); her religiosity, which perfused much of what she did and yet wasn't the excessive godliness he'd experienced with other religious people (Scott even joined her for church on occasion, where he learned that Lori's faith was more one of those new age deals than some sort of ancient piety, and though he didn't care to believe in much of anything himself, he appreciated and understood and respected her desire to); the solidity of her familial upbringing (older brother, older sister, younger brother, industrious father, devoted gentle mother). This stability was what he'd always wanted. It was. It really was.

Ultimately, all the leaves fell from the giant oak tree outside Scott's window, leaving its branches grey and cold and bare and ready for the winter.

Three Weeks Pre Brand-Changing Day, 2012

He'd never been much one for entertainment, R.J. hadn't, but he did own a TV. This evening after he arrived home from his shift at the restaurant and laid his jacket, neatly folded, on the small round breakfast table, he walked into the living room and picked up the remote and turned the TV on. The show that was on looked boring and insipid and like a waste of network dollars. He changed the channel and changed it again several more times before giving up and putting the remote back down, leaving the TV on a network whose programming he couldn't yet identify because it was currently playing an ad for laundry detergent. R.J. already had laundry detergent, and in fact he pulled off the stupid tie he was wearing and the stupid blue dress shirt and tossed them into the hamper in his laundry room, right next to which sat a box of the powdered detergent. In his undershirt and black pants he walked back into the living room and fell into its only chair, a dark green recliner with cigarette burns defining the upholstery.

R.J. lit a cigarette, its light fighting for the position of the stronger source in the room with the light of the television, which flickered at irregular intervals as the electron gun behind the screen threatened to die. The old television had been flickering like that as long R.J. had had it. There were no other lights on in the room, but the light from the kitchen spilled over the kitchen doorway's threshold, casting certain shadows.

The rest of the small apartment looked like this: Dark fake wood paneling throughout the bedroom and living room and laundry room. Gray berber carpet, except in the kitchen and bathroom, which were tiled with the same white-and-light-blue chipped and peeling polyurethane tile. White wallpaper with cardinals around the border in the kitchen. White wallpaper with yellow butterflies around the border in the bathroom. A beige shower curtain. A set of antlers hanging over the old television. In the kitchen a toaster and a two-burner stove and a refrigerator filled with Red Bull and eggs and venison sausage. The antlers above the television the only trophy. A large stand-alone freezer in the laundry room, filled with cuts of meat. A light fixture on the ceiling of each room, the one in the kitchen being the only one on right now. White ceilings marred with nicotine. No windows. The only door the one in the kitchen, which led to a short set of steps that when walked up brought one out next to the driveway. The whole apartment R.J.'s parents' refinished basement.

R.J. hadn't always lived here. He'd helped his dad turn the basement into an apartment unit when he was seventeen. He'd planned on renting it from them maybe, but he was thinking also at the time about going to college, and so there was a possibility that his parents wouldn't be renting the place to him, but to someone else. And so then R.J. got married, is what happened, at only eighteen, to this pretty little waitress at the diner where he'd been a cook since he was twelve despite the fact that when he'd started he'd been under the legal working age and they'd had to pay him under the table and he'd worked there without his parent's knowledge. The marriage had lasted sixteen months, during which time R.J. had become a manager at the diner and he and his wife had gotten an apartment of their own. And then one day he'd woken up and she was gone. He'd hardly known her, truth be told, and he'd hardly missed her then and thought of her rarely now.

He rented the basement apartment from his parents until they moved to Florida just a few years ago, intent on enjoying their retirement away from their increasingly reclusive son, but when they'd left they'd given him the house, and now he still lived in the basement, renting the upper-levels to a couple with a baby. And so R.J.'s income source was threefold—The Grill, where his salary was arguably pathetic for the hours he worked, the house, and a small handful of hunting prizes he managed to win throughout the year. He bought little because he found most things to be superfluous, and so he wasn't wanting for money—he could afford cigarettes and guns and ammunition and car maintenance and what food he didn't get from hunting. He cut his own hair.

He could hear the infant crying upstairs as he sat in the recliner, smoking and watching images on the television.

"How was work?"

Technically, R.J. lived alone in the apartment, but for the last week he'd had increasingly frequent visits from that bear he'd failed to kill at the edge of his buddy's property. "Fine."

"Oh, but come on now. Tell me more about it. Details, Rich, details." The bear wasn't fully *there*. It's like he would drift in and out of the edge of R.J.'s awareness, like a wraith or a ghost.

R.J. sighed. "I don't know."

"Of course you do. You were there. You're a smart man."

R.J. took a drag. A black and white cat danced on the screen, trying to sell him salmon treats.

"Ooh, salmon," the ursine phantom said, his voice dripping

with glee. "Nothing beats real salmon though, and I bet you a thousand bucks those things aren't even made from real salmon. Come on, no bet? Come on, Richie, you know I'm good for it. Oh! Oh! There it is, see! Right at the bottom of the screen, with an asterisk. *Product does not contain real salmon.* Ha!"

R.J. looked for the remote, failing to remember where he'd set it down, but by the time he found it on the end table, the commercial had ended and the programming had transitioned into Leno interviewing Barbara Kingsolver, which seemed an odd fit to R.J., who hardly knew who Kingsolver was.

"Okay, so now where were we? Oh yes, work. Tell me about work tonight, R.J. Tell me about Geoff and Mike and Scott and all those guys. No? Come on. Come *on*, man. You work with the most interesting people."

R.J. turned off the TV, stamped out his cigarette in the ashtray on the table. "I'm going to bed."

"At least tell me about Scott."

"What about him?"

"Him and what's-her-name. Lori. How are they?"

"They broke up."

"*What?* No. Why?"

"I don't know. He . . . cheated on her or something."

"Or something?"

"He cheated on her. With Kara."

"The one with the daughter?"

"Yeah."

"But weren't they already fucking. Like before Scott and Lori started going out."

"Yeah."

"And so what? They just kept on fucking through the whole thing?

"No. I don't know."

"You're an observant guy, Rich. What do you *think* you know."

R.J. stood from the chair and walked toward the bedroom. "I don't care. I'm going to bed."

"I'll just keep talking."

"Fine. From what I overheard, they were sleeping together —"

"Scott and Kara?"

"Yes, Scott and Kara. But then Scott started dating Lori—"

"Right. They started dating at that thing you didn't go to. At the lake."

"Mmhmm. The the thing at the lake. So they started dating and Scott broke it off with Kara. Which, from what I can tell, was fine with her because there were no actual feelings there, just sex. So they stopped and Scott started dating Lori and they were pretty happy."

"Right. Which I never figured out, exactly. They're very different people."

"No. No, it's obvious, isn't it? Why they were together. Scott's like this flawed, messed-up guy, what with his mom and everything, and—"

"What about his mom? You never said anything about his mom."

"I don't exactly know. I just overheard Lori say something to him about his mom one day."

"That's stupid."

R.J. walked into his bedroom, where he turned down the sheets on his bed, which he made every morning with military precision. He took his pants off but left on his undershirt.

"So?" The bear urged.

"So, yeah. So Scott's all messed up, and Lori's all 'I love God and love and people,' and she wants to fix him, but at the same time she obviously wants a little of what he has, his imperfection, because her life is so . . . good."

"I don't buy it."

"No, but it makes sense. Because he wants to be with her for the same reason. Because she's good and he wants that goodness."

"So you mean like the *opposite* reason, is what you mean."

"Fuck off." R.J.'s theory about the bear was that maybe the bear *had* died after he'd shot it—he'd never found it again after he followed it into the woods, after all—and that this was its disembodied spirit, haunting him in representation of all the game whose life he'd taken since his father first took him hunting when he was nine.

"I'm just saying, is all," the bear said. "Please, continue."

R.J. was in bed now. He realized that he forgot to take a piss before sliding in, and that he had to go, but he wondered if maybe he could hold it until morning. He was tired.

"R.J. . . ."

"*Dammit!* Get out of my fucking head!"

"I'm not in your head, R.J. I'm real."

"You're not real. I shot you."

"Finish the story, please."

"No."

"If you don't finish the story then I'm just going to stand here next to your bed all night and keep talking and talking and talking and talking and—"

"So Scott doesn't really love Lori, I don't think. But he wants to. But she doesn't want to sleep with him yet, right? So he says okay, fine, yeah, whatever, that's cool. But then he can't help himself and he fucks Kara again."

"Ah."

"Which, the kid is an idiot. They're all idiots. They've got good things going and they fuck 'em up all the time."

"They sound like idiots to me."

"They are. Fucking idiots."

"What about Geoff? How's he doing?"

R.J. rolled over onto his side, his eyelids heavy. "He's the biggest fucking idiot of them all. He doesn't give a fuck about anybody. He cheated on his wife, you know?"

"You told me."

"Thinks it doesn't matter, that nobody knows. But the whole company heard about it."

"I hate that guy."

"I hate all of them. Every single one." R.J rolled over. "But, you know what? It's not the cheating and the lying that bothers me; it's the apathy. This whole damn world is apathetic to everything."

"That a fact?"

R.J. had forgotten to turn the light off in the kitchen, so it shined through the kitchen doorway, losing strength but managing to cast a dim glow through the crack beneath R.J.'s bedroom door. He could see the strip of light. He stared at it until his eyes closed, the light leaving an impression on the inside of his lids just before he slept. "Hate them all," he mumbled.

He could feel the bear still there beside his bed, watching him, and then he could feel its breath on his skin. Its warm, corporeal breath. It whispered: "Hey, Richie, know what would be fun?"

TWO

To whom it may concern (namely, Geoff McCree),

I'll try to keep this brief, and I'll do my best to get to the point as quickly as possible, but first allow me to air a handful of grievances relating both to you and your lackadaisical performance as the general manager of The Grill's Youngstown location as well as to the generally absurd manner with which the company, i.e. Earl's American Grill Restaurant Group, Inc., chooses to carry out its business operations.

Before I go any further, I should probably point out that I have purchased food from The Grill dozens, if not hundreds, of times, and that therefore I am a repeat paying customer, and ergo this letter qualifies as a customer complaint of sorts and should probably be treated as such. Feel free—in fact, feel encouraged—to hang it on the wall right on the inside of the leftmost doors to the kitchen next to all the other customer comments and below the list of arbitrary and pointless statistics like Tip %, GHI (Guest Hospitality Index or whatever), PGA (which I think has already been claimed as the moniker of some sporting event or something), etc. (Yes, I am aware that my comments may stick out from the others w/r/t grammar, syntax, and basic spelling skills, but I promise not to let this embarrass me.)

First, re: your performance as a general manager.[1] When I first started working for you, I had this impression that you were a decent manager: an okay person, business-savvy, compassionate, and a little paunchy. It turns out that I was less than right on all counts, save for the paunch.[2] You've demonstrated, for example, poor business sense by repeatedly refusing to cut employees during far-less-than-peak hours,[3] by blindly following and ostentatiously praising the business practices of the company for which you work (see below), and by booking reservations for large parties[4] during periods when it's patently obvious that the servers on the floor will be unable to handle said parties without spontaneously combusting, yanking out all their hair, or sitting in the corner, arms wrapped around legs in the fetal position, and weeping,[5] and refusing to have the Bissells[6] fixed or replaced.[7] On the subjects of compassion and your being a decent person, well, the examples are simply too numerous to list,[8] but understand that they are reprehensible, and none of the employees who work under you would treat you with the lack of respect that you constantly show them.

Regarding the above examples, I am willing to offer these words of advice: start caring, if only just a little.

Then there is the company itself. I could go on and on for some many pages about the absolutely ridiculous number of coupons that go out each week (which can only hurt business in the long run and also which effectively propagate the, let's admit it, theft of tips which servers would have made had said coupons not been so munificent), the mandatory and repetitious offer of spicy cheese fondue before a customer has had a chance to ask for even drinks (to which the response is almost always a resounding "NO" often followed fifteen minutes later by an emphatic "Hey, hey you! You didn't offer me the spicy cheese fondue!"), or the fact that the majority of our cooks are not chefs and the majority of our bartenders not mixologists (and even if they are mixologists, they're not allowed to mix drinks in a manner befitting a mixologist, so really what's the point). But these things, as profoundly harebrained as they are, don't bother me nearly as much as the draft beer size/price quandary: we are, beginning today, i.e. Brand-Changing Day, insisting on serving standard draft beers smaller than a pint—a practice which I'm ninety-nine percent certain is disallowed by the laws of the universe—and further, we insist on selling them at prices that would make even the Trappist monks laugh/cry.[9]

But my true concerns lie neither with your managing capabilities nor with any one specific company, but rather I believe the entire concept of the American restaurant chain needs to disappear from our collective consciousness.[10] The food at said chains is bad and often dreadfully unhealthy—packed with chemicals and fillers and unnecessary calories[11]—and the corporate mindset permeates the entire dining experience in a way that is disconcerting. There is a reason I only order steak and salad for my employee meals,[12] and that reason is that I, like any health-conscious semi-educated human person, prefer to eat real food,[13] and there's very little real food on the menu of any corporate-owned dining establishment.[14] And yet I can go right down the street, just a mile or two, to privately owned places like Mojo's or The Upstairs, and get quality food prepared with quality ingredients and sometimes even a little bit of artistic flourish along with good beer and good wine and good cocktails and a kind of atmosphere and heart worth paying for.

And I think that's really what people are looking for—good food and good company—but we live right now in a world that so very often refuses to allow us the time or the means by which to acknowledge our options, to explore our own tastes and needs and desires, and so instead of packing up and heading out in search of great experiences, we latch on to the experiences we think are good—the experiences we've been told are good—or even just the experiences we're used to, the ones we've come to think of as "good enough," and we repeat those same experiences over and over and over again because it's all we know and all we have time to know, and it doesn't matter whether they're actually good at all. This is why we go to casual American chain restaurants, and this is why I've worked in four of them, and this is why I'll never work in one again.

All of this, then, is to say that I hereby submit my two weeks notice. That is, April 17 is the last day that I will be available to you for scheduling.[15]

With thanks,
Scott Pelletier

Brand-Changing Day, 2012

On a normal weekday in most American chain restaurants, shifts are staggered. Suppose, for example, that a restaurant opens for lunch at 11 AM, which The Grill does. In this situation, the openers, usually two servers, depending on the location, will come in sometime around 10:30 or 10:45 in order to complete what is a fairly simple amount of prep work: making coffee and iced tea, slicing lemons, lowering chairs that have been placed upside down on table tops by a cleaning crew the night before, pulling condiments from the cooler, rebuilding the drink machine, etc. Then these opening servers (again, usually two) will take care of any customers that enter the restaurant for the first forty-five minutes or so, alternating so that first the first server gets a table, and then the second, and then the first, and so on. Sometimes, on a particularly busy day, this can get overwhelming for the servers, but during most lunch shifts the volume of customers before noon, when the closing servers go on the floor, is manageable. The Grill follows this near-universal procedure except on days when particularly high lunch traffic is expected—days like Christmas Eve, Easter Sunday (which tends to be especially busy in the morning and early afternoon but downright dead at dinner; the only deader dinner shift is Superbowl Sunday), and brand-changing days.

On The Grill's companywide Brand-Changing Day in mid-2012, five lunch servers were scheduled, and also one bartender, and they were all, except for the bartender, Mike, whose mother was sick or whatever, scheduled to come in at 10:30, all of them, so Geoff McCree could go over a few last-minute "brand reminders" and so they could share equally the inevitably high volume of customers that had heard about the rebranding and the new menu and would come in to check it out at the earliest opportunity, which for most people, Geoff seemed to think—although Scott would hardly have used the word "think" to describe anything Geoff did—was 11:00 sharp on a weekday morning.

Scott was happy to be wearing one of the new uniforms. They were not unlike the old uniforms, except instead of black, collarless t-shirts, the male waiters now wore black button-down dress-shirts. Scott's new shirt was slim and form-fitting, and as he walked into the restaurant, he felt the eyes of Michelle and Kara and Betty on his backside. He was disappointed to see the managers, Geoff and Michael, still wearing the same pastel blue dress shirts and pleated dress pants they'd always worn—it seemed that, while corporate's sense of fashion had advanced, the change had not been a complete one.

And now at 10:30 AM, Brand-Changing Day, Scott and Michelle and Kara and Betty walked through the dining room and to the back of the restaurant, where two POS computers sat side by side and where Geoff and Michael were waiting.

"Good morning," Geoff said, grinning.

Scott refrained from thinking the grin was like a big dumb child's grin.

"We'll let you get to your prep work in just a minute, but first we just want to go over a few things just one more time.

Remind you of some procedures and whatnot. And since it's his last day with us, I thought I'd let Michael do it."

Michael stood straight, holding a piece of paper in his hand. He pushed his round glasses up on the bridge of his nose and looked at the paper. Scott liked Michael even though many of the other employees didn't—most found him old and over-eager and timid and thought his breath smelled bad, and while this was true, Scott had to admit, the man was also sincere and was a better manager than the ones already here, despite his eagerness and timidity, and Scott for one would be a little sad to see him leave, but then again, Scott wouldn't work with him after today anyway, even if Michael *were* staying in Youngstown.

"Good morning," Michael said, his voice cracking. He cleared his throat. "We've, uh, we've got just a few reminders to —"

"Wait. Sorry, I don't mean to interrupt you, Michael," Geoff interrupted, "but where's Josh? He's supposed to be here this morning too."

"Maybe he didn't realize he was supposed to come in early," Michael offered, fiddling with the right frame of his glasses.

"I'm here!" The front door squeaked open, echoing through the mostly empty dining room, and all heads turned toward the front of the restaurant. Joshua Brown was walking hastily through the foyer, past the hostess stand, fumbling with the second topmost button of his shirt. "I'm sorry I's late. I had a early class this morning and there was a accident in fronta the parking garage. I just had to change in my car just now."

"Don't worry about it," Michael said. "I was, um, just about to go over a few reminders about the new procedures. Go ahead and clock in."

Josh approached the POS and hit the key that read CLOCK

IN. The screen hadn't been calibrated in some time, so he had to hit the button three times before the contact registered. He started to enter his employee number, but Geoff interrupted him.

"Wait, wait," Geoff said, his voice deep and gruff and drawling. "What's with that shirt?"

Josh's finger froze above the display. "Whata you mean?"

"What are those lines?"

Josh's shirt was cut slim, hugging his muscular dancer's frame, and on either side of the buttons, running from shoulder to waist through the spot where a breast pocket might be placed —and there were no breast pockets on Josh's shirt—were two clean dark lines. "They're just seams."

There was a hint of dumb amusement on Geoff's face and in his voice. "I've never seen a shirt like that."

"Um, yeah," Josh said, starting to type his employee number again. "Thanks. It's European."

The corners of Geoff's lips seemed to be pulling up of their own accord. "It's ridiculous. I can't let you work in a shirt like that."

"*What?*"

"Yeah, no, I'm sorry." Geoff was actually laughing a little now, snickering. "That's absolutely ridiculous. Do you have another shirt with you?"

"What? No, I ain't got no other shirt."

"Listen, I'll let you go home and change, but you just can't wear that."

"I—"

Scott and Michael and Kara and Michelle and Betty watched what was unfolding. Scott had comments, but he withheld them. It was 10:39.

"Naw, man," Josh said. "You're serious?"

"Uh huh," Geoff said. "One hundred percent. You've got to go home and change into a normal dress shirt."

"Naw," Josh was laughing himself now, but it seemed to Scott to be a frustrated laugh, an expression of disbelief. "Naw, man, I ain't changin'. I'm quitting. I'm out of here."

Joshua Brown was a twenty-four year old African American college student double-majoring in dance and theater. He was born in Brownsville, Brooklyn, to Robert and Tamara Jones, a construction worker and homemaker respectively, and lived there until he was four when his parents both died within only two months of each other—his father from testicular cancer and his mother hit by a car while walking back from the QuikiMart on Dumont. After his parents' deaths, Josh was separated from his two siblings, both younger than he, and thrown into a broken and messy legal system. He had a total of five foster parents in two years, most of whom had been nice enough but overwhelmed by the foster process, with the exception of the Dillards, who were mean and abusive, mostly verbally but occasionally physically, i.e. they often called young Joshua a "piece of shit" and a "little shit" and a "little fuck" and used words like "fuck" and "fucker" and they once hit him hard enough that he fell and hit his head and suffered a concussion, after which they felt bad and took young Joshua to the hospital and admitted everything and broke down crying because they weren't cut out for this, they just weren't cut out for this; it was just so hard being a parent, you see, and Joshua, for his part, was only like six years old when he was with the Dillards, so while he knew something was wrong about the way they treated him, he didn't understand just how wrong it was exactly and that people weren't supposed to treat children this way. And then Josh was transferred one last time, to the custody of Jim and Karen Brown, an interracial couple from Youngstown, Ohio, and they were kind and gentle and adopted Josh on his seventh birthday and saved a generous college fund for him, and he probably could have gone to any of the best performing arts schools in the country—even the Tisch School of the Arts back in New York, which has one of the highest tuitions of any arts college in the country and to which he had once dreamed of being accepted—but his parents had been nearly fifty when they adopted him and were over seventy now, and so Josh, despite their insistence otherwise, had decided to stay in Youngstown and attend Youngstown State and care for his parents because they'd cared for him. Josh had a boyfriend, also a theater major, but had also had a few girlfriends and would date a woman again if he met the right one and all. He'd always suspected that Geoff McCree treated him unfairly because of his race and his sexuality, which he didn't flaunt but didn't hide, either, and as he walked out of The Grill on Brand-Changing Day, wearing a hand-made black shirt purchased on Savile Row during a trip to London just this past summer, he considered suing for discrimination, but in the end, after the events of Brand-Changing Day had passed, he decided against legal action, because leaving The Grill that morning very well might have saved his life—who's to say?

When Josh had stormed out and the foyer door had swung shut quietly behind him (they'd all watched as he tried to slam it, but those sort of big heavy restaurant doors are usually on big heavy hinges that work well and move slowly) they all—

Scott, Kara, Betty, Michelle, even Michael—turned to look at Geoff.

Geoff brought his closed hand to his mouth, cleared his throat. His torso bobbed awkwardly.

"I . . . will have to take care of that later. A shame." He raised his eyes expectantly and nodded at Michael. "Well, then. Go on. What are you waiting for?"

It was 10:41. The server line still needed prepping. The chairs still needed taking down.

"Yes. Yes, of course. Right," Michael said. He adjusted his glasses again and looked down at the paper.

Scott knew only a little of Michael's story. He knew he usually went by Mike, but when he'd arrived at The Grill, he insisted on being called Michael so as not to cause confusion with the very popular bartender. Scott knew Michael was married and had owned a medium-sized grocery store in West Virginia, but the store had closed down last year, a consequence of a still-collapsing economy and an increase in feed prices driving food costs higher and the migration of big-box membership stores like Sam's Club and Costco expanding into even the most rural of areas. Scott knew this was Michael's first foray into restaurant management, and he knew Michael's age and his timidity meant he probably wasn't cut out for this corporate hierarchy stuff.

Michael spoke at the paper. "Just a few reminders: New name tags are in the back, um, and so are the new aprons—we'll get those for you in a moment. There's a . . . Oh, we don't have a bartender until one, so you'll need to get your own drinks—remember, the regular drafts go in the new twelve ounce pilsner glasses. Um, let's see. The new cream cartons haven't come in yet, so we're still using the old ones for today. Also, don't forget your coasters, and even though we have new menu items, we're still asking the guests if they want the cheese fondue. Um, Geoff and I don't want to have to comp any fondues because you forgot to ask. Alright, that's about . . . . Listen, you guys are going to do great today, have fun and—"

"We've got a lot of coupons out today, okay guys?" Geoff interrupted. "That means we're going to be busy. People get excited when we get new menus, so we're going to be very busy all day. I don't want mistakes, okay? Got it? You guys got it? Watch your new training videos. If you're not certified on the new material by next week, I can't put you on the schedule, okay? Okay. Get to work."

Michelle and Betty went in the back to cut lemons and make iced tea. Scott and Kara started taking chairs from the tables. The air in the restaurant was stale, but the air between Scott and Kara was staler.

"That sucks about Josh," Kara said.

"It really does," Scott said. "First Angie, and now Josh."

"Angie was her fault though, mostly anyway. She knows that. I mean, she came to work obviously hungover. Twice."

Scott shrugged. "True."

"But Josh—that was uncalled for, just ridiculous. Geoff clearly picks on him because he's gay—"

"He's bi, I think."

"Yeah, well whatever. You know what I mean. He should sue. We all saw what happened. We'd all back him. At least I know I would."

"Definitely. I definitely would."

Scott moved on to the next table, putting some distance between Kara and himself.

"How *is* Angela doing? Have you talked to her lately?"

"Yes, I have. We've been meaning to get together and hang out. Actually, we're probably going to go to O'Darren's tonight, if you want to come hang out. Mike said he might come too."

Scott nodded. "Cool. Yeah, maybe. Definitely."

"What about Lori, have you heard from her at all?"

Scott flipped a chair over and accidentally placed its leg on his foot. His shoe was thick and it didn't hurt. "You don't have to . . . you don't have to ask about her, okay."

Kara nodded. Scott watched her flip a chair from a table and place it on the floor. The chairs were large and Kara was small, and so the scene might have been comical.

"Okay," Kara said. "Sorry."

"No, no, don't be sorry. It's alright," Scott said. "And no, I haven't heard from her for weeks. Except for, y'know, at work, but she doesn't talk to me. Have you? Heard from her, I mean?"

Kara shook her head. "The same," she said. "Just when we work the same shift, which isn't often anymore, and she doesn't say much to me, either."

Scott wasn't picturing Kara naked. He didn't even have an erection. It's a peculiar phenomenon: when you haven't seen a person naked, you tend to picture them naked every now and then, and when you've seen them naked once, their nakedness is all you can think about, but after you've seen them naked dozens of times and done naked things with them, it loses its novelty, the nakedness.

"Yes, well."

"Well."

The chairs were down. Scott walked back into the bar and picked up the remote for the televisions, turning them on and changing the channel to ESPN. There was no point to ESPN in the morning: two muscular men in expensive pinstriped suits sitting behind a desk, debating banal topics with an enthusiasm that should have been reserved for things like elections or fascinating new medical research, not sports; the same few events from games the night before—football games, basketball games, hockey games, baseball games (never soccer games)—playing over and over and over again, simulated little yellow circles highlighting key players or key plays or pointing out that this, right here, is where the ball was or the puck was at such and such point in the game, when so and so made this game-changing play or this heart-stopping catch, and what the hell were the refs thinking, the stupid refs, making a call like that; commentary being commentated; arguments growing heated; one man in a pinstriped suit saying that the whole thing was ridiculous and another man in a pinstriped suit saying that it was the best thing to happen to the sport in decades; a third man, sometimes, joining in, and this guy would be the only Caucasian on the screen, voicing his opinion tepidly; *comme ci, comme ça;* the commentators and the casters and the arguers all men, rarely women, who couldn't play the sports themselves or who had played long ago but were incapable of doing so now due to age or injury or having enough money now, after a dozen seasons in the game, content to just sit in front of a camera in the morning and argue instead of being part of the legend anymore. But it seemed to Scott the grand tradition of the Corporate American Chain Restaurant that bar televisions be tuned to only sports and sports-related programming, unless of course a customer requested a channel change, in which case the channel was changed as long as nobody else in the area was watching the sports.

Scott looked solemnly around the empty bar. It was quiet and serene in here right now—the lights were low, and the drawl of the college football commentators was monotone and grey. The bar reflected a space somewhere in Scott's chest.

Scott made his way into the back of the house, where the lights were brighter and white and assaulted his pupils harshly. A small Cambro of freshly sliced lemons sat on the stainless steel countertop, the wooden handle of a serrated steak knife jutting upward from them so the servers, when a customer ordered water with lemon or iced tea with lemon, could cut a little slit in the citrusy flesh. Before today, it was standard practice to serve all iced tea or water with a slice of lemon, but with Brand-Changing Day came any number of cost-cutting measures, one of which was the elimination of automatic complimentary citrus.

Michelle and Betty were fiddling with something on their respective breasts. Scott liked them (Michelle and Betty, that is, although their breasts seemed fine, as well)—they were both high-spirited, possessing a bubbliness that wasn't forced and a positivity that Scott wished he could imitate.

"Are those the new name tags?" Scott asked, his voice rising with genuine inquisitive interest.

"Yeah," Michelle and Betty said in unison. Betty winced as the pin poked her skin.

Scott approached the pile of name tags on the counter, sifting through them until he found the one with his name on it. The tags were black with white lettering in a font derivative of Comic Sans, and where the old name tags had had soft, rounded corners, these new ones had obnoxious points, and near these corners, sharp triangular extensions poked from the tag, so that the tags were like rectangles that had collided with a fun-sized starburst.

"They look like shuriken," Scott commented, picking up his tag, which sat next to Josh's, which was still in the pile.

"Like *what*?" Betty asked.

"Shuriken," Scott repeated. "Japanese throwing stars."

"Oh," Michelle said. "You mean like ninja stars." She looked at Betty. "He means like ninja stars."

Scott nodded. "Exactly," he said.

He fingered the tag he'd just pinned to his chest, still sifting through the pile with his other hand. Underneath the names, in small white letters, was printed the word "expert."

"Like fraudulent, misshapen ninja stars."

The lights in the kitchen flickered ominously, and the employees looked up at them reflexively. One of the cooks behind the expo counter laughed, and another, Joe, said, "Shu' the hell up, man! I almost cut myself," which only encouraged the first cook to laugh louder.

Kara came out of the cooler, a bag of lemons in her hand.

"I already cut lemons, honey," Betty said.

Kara saw the plastic container full of lemon wedges. "Oh, you did. Whoops. What's up with the lights?"

Geoff came through the server line, a cordless phone in his hand. "It's the satellite on the roof," he said. "It's loose and the wind is blowing it around and it's screwing with the power cables or something. I put in a service call yesterday."

The phone rang and Geoff held it to his ear, disappearing through the door with the YES on it and into the lobby.

It was 10:57. The hostess had arrived when no one was looking, and Scott could see her through the window of the double doors with the YES on them, standing near the front doors, organizing the menus and talking with Michael, who looked even older from this distance, the light from the late-morning sun shinning on them both through the front doors' windows, bathing them in soft yellows.

* * *

Geoff's day was continuing to go south. It had started, of course, when he'd spilled that grease from his breakfast sandwich, burning his arm and staining his shirt. And now he'd lost a server on what was probably going to be the busiest day, sales-wise, of the year. But what choice did he have, though? He couldn't let his employees run around his restaurant in some queer shirt—it was against the new uniform code, and it looked damned silly. He hadn't expected Josh to quit, though, but maybe it was for the best—the kid wasn't exactly the sort of person Geoff wanted representing his restaurant, giving off certain impressions to his customers. It wasn't that Geoff had received any specific complaints, but he knew what people were thinking when Josh approached their table.

And so now he needed to find a replacement, someone to pick up a lunch shift, and fast. He needed only to worry about today for the moment; he would cover the rest of the shifts Josh's departure had left unfilled on the schedule later.

Geoff sat in the office, holding the phone and flipping through the antiquated Rolodex on the table. So much of the information was out of date: there were names and numbers in here for employees who had left long ago, and the cards were arranged in no particular order. Angela, Mark, Chris, Ted, Bev (who had been attracted to Geoff, Geoff had always sort of suspected a little), Betty, Lori, Tom . . . *Wait.* Geoff flipped back. Lori still worked here—she was the blonde girl with the curly hair. Geoff dialed the number on the card with the thumb of his right hand.

Twice it rang, and then a third time. A fourth. "Hello."

"Hi, yeah, this is Geoff from The Grill—"

"—You've reached Lori Bristol's iPhone. I'm not available right now, but leave me a message and I'll call you back. Jesus loves us all."

There was a beep. Geoff might have sighed, but he left a message and returned to flipping through the Rolodex.

He called several more employees. He called the servers who would be working tonight, hoping someone might be willing to pick up a double shift. He called Mike, the bartender, who was already scheduled to come in this morning but would be late, hoping to convince him to come in sooner than planned. He even called Michelle before remembering she was already here—he hung up the phone, feeling dejected (another one of those words). In a period of ten minutes, he'd left seven brief messages on various voicemails. Perhaps someone would call back and tell him they could come in. For now, he would have to make do with four servers instead of five.

The lights flickered. *Dammit.*

Geoff took the phone with him when he left the office. He'd have to call the electrician again—if the lights went out for good, it wouldn't matter how many servers he had on the floor. He walked into the kitchen. There was a small pile of dirty prepware at the dish station. Eddie would be in at noon.

"What's up with the lights?" Geoff heard someone, one of the girls, say as he crossed the server line. He told them about the loose satellite dish.

The phone rang in his hand, its ringtone two short, deep electronic squawks followed by one higher, longer one. He held the phone to his ear as he entered the front of the house. Thank God, someone was calling back. He didn't bother to glance at the caller ID screen. "Hullo?"

"Geoff."

"Yeah, listen, thanks for calling me back. Can you cover a shift for me, this morning, actually? It's last minute—"

"Geoff, it's Elaine."

The indignity of the fact that he failed to initially recognize his wife's voice was lost on Geoff. "Oh, sorry. What's going on?"

"I . . . I tried your cell phone, but—"

(Sometime around ten o'clock, Geoff had been in the office, printing out customer comments that had come through to the store via email. He'd printed half of the second email—a lengthy complaint about long wait times for the customer's food, which had then been cold when the customer finally received it, or so the customer said in the email—but the printer had run out of ink before printing the third page. Geoff had spun around in his chair, swinging towards the small supply closet by the door to get more paper, and his elbow had crashed into his full coffee cup with malice. His cell phone's screen had turned white and the device grew warm before shutting off completely. He'd tried turning it back on and plugging it into the charger, but there had been no response on the phone's part.)

"Geoff, my water broke. It's time."

Geoff was quiet for a moment. He was standing by the bar, sort of leaning up against it, and he noticed that a few of the new pilsner glasses, which were stacked three high behind and around the tap, had smudges on them, likely created by whoever had unboxed and stacked them. He would need to tell Mike to polish them when he arrived.

"Geoff, are you listening—"

"No, I heard you. Your water broke. Listen, I can't leave here right now, though. It's Brand-Changing Day and—"

"Of course. No, right. I wouldn't expect you to leave."

"Can your sister or someone . . ."

"I already called her. She'll be here in just a few minutes to take me to the hospital."

There was a certain wrongness to the fact that his wife had felt it prudent to call her sister before her husband, but Geoff didn't relate well to wrongness, and so it hardly registered on his consciousness. "Great, good. How soon do you think you'll have the baby?"

"I don't *know*! Gee, let's see, given my prior experience with having babies . . ."

"Yeah, right, that was a dumb question. Listen, I'll get to the hospital as soon as I can."

"I'm sure."

"I will. I have to go now, though, we open . . ." There were three customers at the hostess stand. The hostess, whose name he didn't know, was smiling and making small talk as she counted out menus. "We're open now, actually. I gotta go. I'll call you back, or your sister. I'll call you to check up soon."

The line clicked off before Geoff could end the call himself.

Scott approached the table with four of the little round coasters with the picture of Sam Adams Boston Lager on them, one for each of the three customers at the first table of the day and one extra that he hadn't meant to grab but did because the coasters tended to stick together when fresh from the packaging. He placed the coasters to the right of each of the three men, tucking the fourth into the large pocket on the front of his apron. (The old aprons had had three smaller pockets, which made separating their contents—e.g. cell phone, cash and change, order book, straws—a cinch.)

"Gentlemen," Scott said, the smile on his face genuine and

his hand searching the pocket for one of the pens he brought to work. He always brough five, but when he needed them, he had a hard time finding even one. "How's everybody doing today?"

(Many people, Scott had observed, said, "How are *we* doing today?" which Scott thought was a dumb way to phrase the question: he knew how he was doing, and thus he knew how part of the we was doing, and so it didn't make sense to say "we" because he lacked knowledge of only the current state of "they.")

They were clearly businessmen—they wore dark pinstripe suits, bold, solid-colored ties, and had styled their hair with greaseless pomades, creating that sort of *GQ* side part and coif. The one with his back against the window, sitting on the opposite side of the table from where Scott stood, had a greying ten-day beard, but aside from that the men looked young— thirty, maybe thirty-five.

The one with the beard, without looking up from his menu, said unceremoniously, "Just a Sprite."

As a general rule, Scott started each shift with an attitude based in phlegmatic optimism. He genuinely enjoyed interacting with other people—attractive single women, well-behaved children, kindly elderly couples who had been married for fifty years, and especially smart people, the sort of people he aspired to join at the top of the business world some day—but when faced with the sort of customer who didn't understand how to continue the natural flow of a basic conversation, how to respond to pleasantries and traditional greetings, Scott's optimism withered fast. What had once been a bunch of juicy green grapes of sanguineness was now just a single bullish raisin.

"Of course," Scott said, his smile still present but its genuineness less so. "Sprite it is. And for the rest of you gentlemen?"

The man to Scott's left, whose tie was dark blue and thin, afforded Scott the courtesy of looking up as he ordered. "Just a Coke for me is fine," he said.

"And, uh . . . I guess I'll take a Sprite too," the third man said, his eyes down.

Scott wrote the drinks on his order pad in sequence the men were sitting, starting on his left: Coke, Sprite, Sprite. He could easily remember the three drinks, but since the servers were required to hand in all their order slips at the end of the shift (they were told the managers compared order slips with final receipts to check for accuracy, but Scott didn't believe this ever happened), he might as well write it now anyway.

"Sounds good," Scott said. "I'll be back with those in just a moment, but first—" and here was the most ludicrous part of the serving procedure "—would any of you like to start with an appetizer? Perhaps our delicious spicy cheese fondue."

The men each looked up at him now, their faces blank. The cheese fondue was disgusting—greasy and lukewarm and served with mass-produced brittle corn chips—and it was as if the businessmen could see through Scott's disingenuous offering of it.

As he returned to the kitchen to fetch the customers their drinks, Scott remembered fondly one of the most amusing drink orders he'd ever witnessed: It hadn't happened to Scott himself, but he'd been standing at the very next table when one of his coworkers at Groovy Burger, whose name Scott honestly and guiltily could never remember, but which might have been Tony, approached a recently sat middle-aged couple. "My name is ———," he said. "What can I start you folks off to drink with today?"

"What do you have?" the middle-aged man asked.

"Well," the server started, "we have Coke products—"

"I'll have a Pepsi," the woman interrupted.

"Fuck. You."

Scott had nearly choked. The section of the restaurant in which he'd been standing went silent. Interestingly, the server whose name Scott could not remember was not fired; his fiancé had broken off their engagement the day before and his car had been hit by a pickup truck on the way to work that morning, so the manager took pity on him and told him to pull himself together and suspended him for a week.

Scott placed a Coke and two Sprites on his tray, again in the order in which the businessmen were sitting, the smile on his face once again genuine and this time possessed of humor.

"Do you gentlemen have any questions about the new menu? Anything I can help you with?"

The one with the beard took a sip of his Sprite. "Yeah," he said. "This here, this 'Create Your Own Garden Bar,' what is that? Like a salad bar?"

"Um, yes." Scott fiddled with the order pad in his hands. "I'm told . . . they tell us that all of The Grills are going to be getting salad bars. In fact, most of them already have, but ours isn't scheduled to be installed until next week."

The man frowned. "So what you're telling me is you don't have this yet."

Scott shook his head. "No, we don't. We will soon."

The frown morphed into a scowl. "Give me this grilled chicken salad then. No croutons. And for *fuck's sake* please tell me you have fat-free ranch."

"Sure," Scott lied. "I can bring you fat-free ranch. And for you?"

Closing his menu, the man with the blue tie looked at Scott. "Bacon cheeseburger. Medium. No mayo. And, uh . . . give me some fries. No wait . . . do you have loaded . . . nah, that's okay. Fries are fine."

Scott wrote the order down, circling "no mayo" so he wouldn't forget to specify it on the POS.

The man with the greying ten-day beard glared at the man with the blue tie. "Dude . . ."

The man with the blue tie shrugged at his friend indignantly. "Dude."

Scott turned to the third man, tapping his pen on his order pad. "And for you, sir?"

"How's that new chicken rogan josh?"

Scott's demeanor relaxed. While he found the idea of a casual American chain restaurant serving Indian dishes—the training material for the new menu called it "Indian Infusion"; there was also a fish curry and a samosa appetizer on the new menu—laughable, he had to admit he was surprised, when he'd tasted it, to find the chicken rogan josh more than palatable. "It's actually quite good," he said.

"Give me that, then."

"Okay. No problem."

"But I want my chicken crispy."

"I'm sorry . . ."

"Yeah, crispy, y'know?"

"It's grilled chicken, though, sir."

"Yeah, I know that. That's fine. Just make sure the grilled chicken is crispy."

"I . . ." Scott silently reminded himself that he wouldn't have to deal with idiotic orders like this after today. "I'll see what I can do."

He walked to the POS system furthest from the table where his customers were sitting, tray and pen and order pad held loosely at his side, a vexed groan and a childish whimper meeting somewhere in his throat and threatening to spill out into a vocal display of his annoyance. He tapped lightly on the dark computer screen, which was smudged and at first unresponsive, and so he stabbed at it more harshly with his finger until it finally sprung to life. He rang in the order: grilled chicken salad (no croutons), bacon cheeseburger (medium, sans mayo), fries, and under NEW MENUE (sic.—the word was curiously and frustratingly misspelled on the recently updated POS), chicken rogan josh. There was no spiciness level option for the rogan josh —the cooks used a pre-made curry paste that was delivered in the same sort of bags as the soup. Scott's finger hovered above the screen, hesitated, before tapping SPECIAL INSTRUCTIONS. He typed slowly on the barely responsive onscreen keyboard: "Crispy grilled chicken." If there was a question mark key, he would have used it.

Folding his order pad closed, he picked up the tray and carried it into the kitchen, tossing it on the stainless steel counter next to the iced tea machine and lemons. He placed his elbows on the expo counter.

"Yo, Scott!" Joe called. Ticket in hand, he turned away from the grill and toward the expo counter.

"I know—" Scott started to say.

"Hell's this mean? 'Crispy grilled chicken.' Hell is that?"

Scott sighed. "I don't know. He—"

"They want like fried chicken or something? I don't think that'd taste very good, man."

"No, no. He wants grilled."

"Hell? That's boneless skinless breast, man, which already

tastes like, like rice cakes or some'in'. Wha's he expect me to do?"

"Just burn it or something. I mean, don't burn it, but cook it a little longer."

"That'll be dry as hell." Joe turned to the cook on the line. "Yo, Chuck, give me that chicken well done. No, not for the salad—the chicken for the rogan josh. God, stupid mother . . .'"

Kara walked into the kitchen then. She nudged her shoulder toward the grill. "What's his problem?"

"Just a stupid order," Scott told her. The time was 11:21.

It was 11:57 when the phone rang again. The backlit neon screen illuminated, displaying a number Geoff didn't recognize; the ringer blared its three-toned ring, whose shrillness startled Geoff aright. He'd been in the office, sitting in the chair, his eyes drifting closed of their own free will. There were fewer customers so far than he'd expected—one table per server, which is to say, four tables.

"Hello," Geoff said into the cordless receiver.

"Geoff? Where the hell are you?"

Geoff rubbed his eyes with his free hand. "Who is this?"

"What do you mean "Who . . ."? It's your goddamn sister-in-law, Geoff. Where are you?"

"Marla?"

"Yes, *Marla*. Listen, Geoff, you better tell me you're on your way to this hospital right now. Your wife is in severe pain, Geoff. Do you hear me? The doctors don't know what's going on, but there's some sort of problem. Do you hear me, Geoff? Something is wrong with your wife! With the baby! Are you still at the restaurant?"

"Yeah, I'm—"

"Get the hell over here! Elaine is asking for you, and I'm telling her you're coming."

The line clicked off. Geoff had yet to end a phone call himself today.

The chilliness of the day and the gustiness of the air had conspired against Mike the Bartender to induce in him a mighty fine hankering for a cigarette. He'd been struggling for months now to once and for all quit the habit, abandoning the tar-and-nicotine toxicant for first a day, and then a week, and then two weeks, each time making it longer without a drag but each time failing inevitably and smoking a pack or two in a day—like a binge-eater, or more like a warrior who fights and fights on an empty stomach before loading up on calories during a few moments' peace—before vowing again that this time would be the last. Half-way through his journey to an addiction-free life, he'd stopped smoking marijuana, not because he'd ever been addicted to it (few pot-smokers ever are), but perhaps because the feeling of that rolled-up paper between his fingers was too familiar, too much of a reminder for the tiny part of the lizard brain he wanted to quash for good.

And but the air was cold and moving swiftly, and Mike knew it deep in his amygdala that a good long smoke would warm him up nicely; fortunately, he had neither cigarette nor lighter on his person as he stepped out of the driver's seat of his black Scion xD, and he hadn't touched either in over a month now, and he'd lost fifteen pounds in that month, and, though his meditations weren't as deep as they'd once been, they were clear and more serene, and he wasn't about to reject those benefits just for the sake of a little temporary warmth. He entered through the restaurant's front double doors.

He'd received Geoff's message a little over an hour ago, and knowing it was unlikely anyone else would come in at such short notice, and since he was supposed to be in at one anyway, and since his mother's doctor's appointment had taken less time than either of them had anticipated (the doctor had been worried: Mike's mother had been suffering from mild-to-severe pain in her side for nearly a week now, and she might have had a pancreatic tumor, the doctor said, but it was impossible to know for sure unless he took some scans, and so he did a CT and what he found was a cracked rib, and Mike's mother started laughing, even though it hurt to laugh, because she'd been out with her bowling league last week and during her turn had slipped on the greased-up floor of the lane, her legs ejecting backwards from beneath her body in rather comic style, her right arm yanked forward and up by the weight and pendular motion of the 20-pound bowling ball, so that her body was parallel to the floor, and she'd fallen just like that, landing in a prone position, bruising the edge of her chin, and somehow it hadn't even occurred to her that she might have injured her rib, and, oh, how mightily silly), he figured he'd just come in as early as possible, which was now, at noon.

"Hey, Mike," the hostess said.

Mike smiled. He always smiled. He'd seen the hostess smoking before, and he thought about asking her for a cigarette.

"Mike." Michael nodded at him.

"Michael." Mike nodded back. "Busy?"

Michael shook his geriatric head. "Not in the slightest. We've had four tables come in in the last hour—there are like maybe ten guests in the whole place right now. And no bar guests, by the way, so."

Mike laughed. A short, curt laugh. Like "Hah." Of course that's how it would work: he would come in early—or at least as early as one who was originally supposed to be late can be—and there would be almost no customers. But oh well.

He walked back behind the bar, which was indeed devoid of customers, and removed the grey knit scarf he'd been wearing. He clocked in on the bar POS and turned around and saw smudges on several of the new pilsner glasses. He picked up a white bar towel and began polishing. (As a rule, bartenders at The Grill weren't required to wear aprons, which didn't wholly make sense, because bartenders and servers performed many and most of the same duties involving food and drink and moving about the restaurant, but which was a good thing in this case, because yesterday Mike had been given the new button-down shirts bartenders were now required to wear, which, unlike the new server dress code, were very specific, company-made shirts with the word "mixologist" embroidered in red Comic Sans on the back and which, Mike realized as Michelle walked by, giving him a wave and a "hello", had the same striped pattern as the new aprons, and wearing the shirt with the apron—that is to say, with stripes on top and stripes on bottom—would have looked utterly tacky. So good judgment call on corporate's part there.)

"I'm sorry, but the Verizon Wireless customer you are trying to reach is not accepting calls at this time."

Geoff willed R.J. to turn back on his phone, which obviously off, but as a man of little will to begin with, Geoff's telepathic powers were lacking. Why would R.J. turn his phone off on a day like today—*Brand-Changing Day* for chrisakes!—anyway?

Geoff was surprising himself immensely; he hadn't in many years experienced internal emotional outbursts like the one he was now experiencing. He took a breath—a small, shallow breath that wouldn't have done even a suffocating man any good—and thought. He couldn't leave the restaurant right now—it was slow at the moment, but all those coupons were out; things were going to pick up quickly any moment; he could feel it; he was always right about these things (he was rarely right about these things)—not even with Michael here. The man wasn't technically a manager yet, not for another day—there was no way he could run a store on his own, especially once the inevitable wave of customers started showing up. Geoff would have to stay. His wife would have to wait. There was nothing he could do about it.

The phone rang again, and Geoff could feel the sound in his hand as he clenched the phone impossibly tight. He brought it to his ear so fast that he bumped the hard plastic against the side of his head. "R.J.?"

"No, goddammit Geoff! It's Marla. They're taking Elaine in *now*."

"Taking her where?"

"A caesarean, Geoff. A c-section! Do you know what that is? They're going to cut your wife open to get the baby out, do you hear me?"

"A c—"

"Oh you fucking idiot. Yes, a goddamn c-section! Where the hell are you? Are you on your way here? You had better be pulling into the parking lot of this fucking hospital right fucking now, Geoff."

"No, I'm—"

"You fucking bastard. You *bastard*. Your wife might die, Geoff. My sister and your *child* both might die any minute now. Does that concern you in the slightest?"

Geoff ran a heavy, calloused hand through his greasy hair. "Of course it concerns me, Marla. What kind of question is that? But . . . it's Brand-Changing Day—I can't just leave the restaurant unattended. I could lose my job."

"Your *job*? You're about to lose your *family*!"

"I understand that. I'm trying to get someone in here—"

A man's deep, gruff voice came on the phone then. "Geoff. Listen here you fuckin' prick. I told my daughter the day you were engaged what a fuckin' mistake she was makin'. I am going to kill you myself if you don't get your lazy ass over here to this fuckin' hospital. You hear me, *son-in-law*? You're fuckin' dead today if my daughter dies and you ain't here. You're dead today."

Geoff hung up the phone this time. There was a clashing in his mind, like cymbals and drums and fireworks at a half-time show. He wanted to be with his wife right now, he honestly did, but he had a responsibility to this restaurant. Some things were more important than others—why couldn't people see that? If he wasn't needed here, if it weren't Brand-Changing Day, he'd be at the hospital right now.

He dialed R.J.'s number again. A new recording this time.

"I'm sorry, but the number you have called has been disconnected. This is a recording. If you believe you are hearing this message in error, please check the number, hang up, and try again."

* * *

The businessmen were still there, their plates long ago emptied and stacked and pushed to the edge of the table and taken away by Scott, their drinks refilled three or four times, coffee brought with the little creamer packets to the table, and while he despised the men on the basis of their neediness (the one with the burger had asked for three separate condiments three separate and successive times), their ill manners (the bearded one had taken cell phone calls, at least two that Scott had witnessed, right there at the table, his Chris Brown ringtone interrupting the conversation and him yammering into the mobile phone), and their obnoxious attempts at humor (the man with the rogan josh had asked Scott, when he brought their meals, why he hadn't offered the spicy cheese fondue and could they get one for free now, and Scott had glared at them, and they had held his gaze before cracking smiles and laughing raucously), he was grateful for their presence, because in the hour and fifteen minutes since the restaurant had opened, each of the servers had only had one table, and so these men might be Scott's only hope at tips during an otherwise boring lunch shift.

"Yo, Mike," Scott said. "You're early."

Mike was standing behind the bar, polishing pilsner glasses, his gaze focused upward on the television and its repetitious sports commentary. He turned toward Scott. "Hey, man. What's up?"

"You're here early."

"Yes, well, Geoff called, asked if I could, and, well, I could, so I did."

"Ah, probably because Josh quit."

"*What?*"

"Yeah. Seriously."

Mike put the glass with the other clean ones and tossed

the towel on the counter behind the bar. "What the hell happened?"

"Geoff made fun of his shirt," Scott said as if it was only a small thing, and in a sense it was, because everyone knew Josh would get fed up and quit eventually. Scott nodded at the TV. "What are they talking about?"

"Paterno."

"*Still?*"

Mike shrugged.

Scott shook his head, tapping the bar with his fingers.

"So," Mike said, "did you actually write it?"

Scott nodded, reaching into his back pocket and withdrawing the four folded pieces of white paper, which, other than the creases, were in perfect condition, and handed them to Mike. "Yeah. It's a little long."

Mike unfolded the pages and read them quickly but thoroughly. "Holy wow, man. That's brilliant. I mean *brilliant.*"

At an earlier point in his life, Scott might have beamed. "Thanks," he said coolly. "I'm not much of a writer, but I'm proud of it."

"How many words?"

"With footnotes? I don't know—like two thousand."

"Ha!"

Mike refolded the pages and gave them back to Scott, who placed them back into his pocket, tucked safely between his wallet and his cheek.

"You know you'll be so fired for that, though," Mike said.

Scott nodded once, a self-assured nod. "I'm leaving tomorrow anyway, so."

Mike nodded too. "Ah. Where?"

Scott shrugged. "I don't really know yet. My things are in a bag; I'll buy a bike and see where life takes me, I suppose."

"I'm a little envious," Mike said. "A lot, actually. I'd love to do something like that, but I've got my Ma. So, what about Lori? Have you told her?"

Scott shook his head. "No. She doesn't need to know. In fact, she's better off not knowing."

"You guys could have been great together, man."

Scott took a breath, a deep, warm breath. "Yeah, well, I had hoped so, but . . . I fucked that up."

Scott looked up now at Kara, who was standing at a table by the window, a basket of garlic cheese biscuits in her hand and a smile on her face, talking to a middle-aged lady in a pink sweater who was eating with an elderly man. In the literal sense, it was Kara Scott had fucked, again and again and again, in a dozen different ways, and not because he loved her or wanted her, but because she came to him each time, and sometimes they were a little drunk, like that first time in the shower, but more often they were sober and aware and felt dirty and wrong afterwards, Scott because of his infidelity and Kara because of her part in it, and then they'd do it again the next week or the next night or immediately.

Scott wondered how he always did this, always screwed things up, each time in a different and epic way. It was like every year was a reinvention. It was like when he'd been watching *Doctor Who* with Lori, how The Doctor regenerated after dying: he was still the same person—somehow, he was still the same person—but his body was different and his face was different and his personality changed in tiny little infinitely noticeable ways. It was like that, except it happened far more frequently, and while there had only been like a dozen Doctors, there had been many dozen Scott Pelletiers, and there was a new one every three or six or nine months. But every Scott was the same Scott, was the thing, only slightly different than the previous incarnation. His body changed and grew and hardened as he pushed it to perform new feats and lift new weights and brave new conditions. His feelings changed and his opinions grew and reshaped themselves, and he moved to new places and saw new things and met new people. And he every time did his best to guide the process, to effect the change that was inevitable, to mold the growth and toning and the restructuring of heart and mind and body. And then but now here he was, just like every time, working in a restaurant and taking orders and pretending that it was what he wanted. And yes, the restaurant was darker this time. The apartment was smaller than last time. The women were the prettiest and smartest and realest he'd ever met. And Scott's shoulders were broader than they were ten months ago, just like his quads were firmer than they'd been a year before that. Scott's hair was longer and his beard nonexistent (he'd played with growing a beard before, in Pittsburgh). His mother was deader and his father was far more behind bars than he'd ever been. And of course, Scott was probably also more in love than the last time or the time before that or the time before that. But still. And besides, he'd screwed the love part up too. Every other shift, every other regeneration, had birthed a slightly better Scott. At least, he'd felt like a better Scott each time, if only by virtue of the differentness and the movement. He'd gone from San Diego to Youngstown and there, when he was old enough, he got a job at a restaurant, and it was progress because he was getting older and it was *a job*. And then he grew bored with that one, and he got another one, at a different restaurant. And this second job was at a restaurant still, yes, that was true, but it was at a *better* restaurant, and he was making more money and more friends. And he grew some more and realized that this city just wasn't the city he needed anymore—he'd outgrown this city—and so he moved to a bigger city, and he loved it for nearly a year, and even though he was still working in a restaurant and it was the same chain he'd been working at in Youngstown, it was in a *bigger city*, and he had his *own place*, and his place was *big and comfortable* and it was *full of furniture and things*. And then he'd quit the restaurant there, because he was confident that *now was the time*, that he was growing again and learning, and he wanted nothing more than to grow and learn all day, and if he just kept growing and learning, he'd be fine, he'd become a new Scott and the new Scott would sustain him every time. He'd—and it really was the perfect metaphor even if he hadn't known it until now thanks to Lori Bristol—regenerate. Which he did. But somehow, though, his last regeneration hadn't gone as he'd anticipated, had it? Because now here he was, and, yes, maybe it was a new restaurant that he worked at now, but it was a restaurant. And it was in an old city, too, a smaller one where he'd been before, and how had that happened? He was less one mother, too, which certainly felt like a step backward, and which was cruelly ironic, because last time he'd grown, when he'd moved away, that Scott felt like he was ready to be without a mother and so he'd left and gone away, and now this Scott didn't know what he was supposed to do without her. It was all so wrong, and he knew that it was wrong, had known the entire time despite his arrogance and his self-assurance. And another reinvention was happening, too. It was happening now. He didn't know if he was going to step back or forward, but he had to step again.

Scott looked back at Mike. "Lori doesn't need to know I've gone until after I've gone. It'll be better for her that way."

The next hour was the busiest of the lunch shift. The businessmen stayed until 1:15, and they tipped Scott better than he would have expected. He had five more tables between 12:30 and 2:00—a young mother and her two toddler sons, a woman and a man obviously in the throes of some secret liaison, four middle-aged women dressed well and drinking white wine with lunch and laughing garishly at each other's jokes, two new mothers out with their sleeping infants, a man with greying hair who sat by himself and read the news on a generic plastic tablet —which meant that each of the other servers had five more customers also (except for Betty, whom the hostess skipped at one point, and Mike, who as a bartender wasn't part of the seating rotation). At one point, Geoff, whose otherwise dry voice sounded like it wanted to crack, said to Scott, "I think we have an influx of people coming in," and Scott wanted to reply sharply, because what *else* could an influx possibly be doing?, but he kept his mouth shut and nodded agreeably. Over the course of the morning and afternoon, Scott made an even thirty-four dollars.

"I need runners! I need runners and help runners."

Mike resisted the urge to cover his ears at the shrill exclamation, the desperate call for assistance. The time was 1:15 and he had no tables, but everybody else did. He sipped at his Diet Coke and marveled at how he'd come to hate the stuff in recent weeks, how he'd seriously come to utterly despise it's sickeningly sweet, dreadfully artificial taste, its syrupy consistency, its sappy texture. He used to like Diet Coke, like really used to *like* it, like he drank it all the time and didn't care so much about the taste because he couldn't so much taste it. But now—but now he could taste, like could really *taste* it, and it was gross, disgusting even, and so he took one more sip and coughed and gasped and wanted to vomit. He actually wanted to vomit. But he didn't vomit, and he walked over to the garbage can by the pass and held the Styrofoam cup over it in his right hand and squeezed, and the cup sort of—if it had been a glass cup, which is to say a glass, it would have shattered and cut his hands and he even might have bled a little or a lot—it sort of just collapsed in between the heel of his palm and his fingers. His middle finger even went through the cup, through the Styrofoam, and so followed his ring finger and his index finger as he kept squeezing. The Diet Coke, sticky and sick and cold, poured from the holes in the cup and dripped off his fingers and the side of his palm and down his right arm. Some of it had even spurted from the pressure of the squeeze and splashed up and onto his face, and so it also dripped from his face.

They weren't supposed to use the Styrofoam cups, which were for children and take-out orders and burning with the goal of releasing toxic chemicals into the atmosphere, but instead management bought them those little paper cups that you might find in an office by the water cooler or that a dentist might give you after an uncomfortable and way-too-personal cleaning so that you could wash the fluoride out of your mouth. Mike never used the little paper cups, though, one reason being that they reminded him of the fluoride, which he never liked and which no one ever really likes, he knew, because it's always either cherry which doesn't taste like cherry or some weird flavor like maybe chocolate which if the cherry doesn't taste like cherry, then the chocolate certainly doesn't taste like chocolate, and another being that they could only fit one ice cube and an ounce of any given liquid (or two ounces of the liquid if you didn't care about temperature and were willing to forego the ice cube, which Mike wasn't because he liked his Diet Coke cold) and this made Mike feel like he was doing shots like some underage girl in a bar every time he got a drink at work, which was silly because he didn't even drink alcohol. At all. And he didn't smoke anymore either.

"You okay, man?" Scott asked. Scott had heard the call for runners and had walked into the kitchen through the big YES door just in time to witness Mike's little miniature breakdown.

"Yeah," Mike said, shaking a little even as he answered. He started to wipe his hand on his apron but was tending bar this shift and therefore wasn't wearing one. "I don't like Diet Coke anymore," he said as he walked over to the sink nearest the trash can by the pass. He ran the tap and rinsed the sticky brown residue from his hand and arm. He stared at it as it fell into the sink and diluted with the water that washed it down the drain. There were no paper towels in the paper towel dispenser, which according to the Ohio Public Health Code, was a serious violation.

"Yeah, but who does?" Scott patted him on his bearish back and walked away.

Mike took a moment to stand completely still. He took a deep breath and centered himself.

At 2:20, the restaurant was nearly empty again. Two tables lingered a little longer, talking animatedly and drinking coffee (one of the customers even commented on the coffee, which was a new blend and better than the one The Grill had been brewing before Brand-Changing Day, was this particular customer's opinion), but even they were gone by 2:30, and Geoff, who walked the dining room clutching the cordless phone in an endless death grip, sent the hostess and one of the two cooks home and cut Michelle and Betty from the floor. He watched as they cleaned their sections, pulling out tables and running the Bissell across the floor, filling salt and pepper shakers and sugar caddies, straightening the blinds that small children had left in disarray, while Mike and Scott and Kara and even Michael, who had asked Geoff a little bit ago if he was feeling okay—you look a little pale, and you're sweating—hovered around the bar, engaged in expressive conversation.

Geoff should have been gone by now—R.J. should have arrived half an hour ago—but he was still here, still clutching and clutching harder with each passing moment. He'd called his sister-in-law back repeatedly, hoping to secure an update on his wife's condition, on the surgery, on his child, but she refused to answer, either because she was in the hospital or because she was angry with him for not rushing to his wife's side.

They didn't understand: he had a restaurant to run; he had responsibilities that outweighed other concerns; it was his job to make the place run smoothly and efficiently, and it would be wrong to just leave, to leave it all in the hands of someone new and inexperienced. These, *this*, here and now, this building and these changes, were the important things in his life. They always had been. But as he stood, watching Mike place two straws in his ears, sticking out his tongue and wrinkling his nose as everyone laughed and Kara smacked him on the shoulder, something inside Geoff that he'd been holding onto for the last decade finally left him. He was kidding himself. No one important was coming in today. It had hardly been busy for lunch, one of the slowest days in a very long time. Maybe he should give up and give in and go.

"No, I'm a moose!" Mike said, wiggling the straws and wagging his dangling tongue back and forth.

"What the hell kinda moose is that?" Kara said, and they all laughed at Mike's wingy sense of humor. Moments like this were not uncommon at The Grill, and Scott would admittedly miss them.

"So, shouldn't R.J. be here?" Michelle asked, wandering up to the bar, Betty behind her, both with stacks of receipts and wads of cash in hand.

Michael scratched his chin, which had only just a few wrinkles. He nodded. "Geoff told me he was coming in at two. I don't know if that changed or—"

"It didn't change," Geoff interrupted, joining the group at the bar, which he seldom did. He held up the black cordless phone, greasy with the sweat of his palm. "I've been trying to get a hold of him for a while now, find out what's up, but his number's disconnected. Have any of you heard anything?"

They each shook their heads. They never heard from R.J. outside of the restaurant, except when he was working and they were off and he needed to call one of them about a scheduling change, but even then his phone encounters were curt and pithy and dry.

Michael reached into his pocket, pulling out his five-year-old flip-style cell phone. "No messages," he said, looking at Geoff. He shrugged. "I don't know."

"We're ready to be cashed out," Michelle said to Geoff, speaking for she and Betty.

Geoff nodded, but then the phone vibrated in Michael's hand, and he looked down at the screen, his face suddenly crestfallen.

"R.J.?" said Geoff.

Michael shook his head. "No. It's a text from . . . you know Cathy from Jamestown?"

Geoff swallowed. "Um, yup. I wasn't aware you knew her."

"Yeah, well, it's a text message from her. She says . . . well, apparently, Earl Bradford died last night."

Mike's eyes grew wide. Kara frowned. Geoff's face showed no expression. Scott said, "The CEO?"

Michael nodded. "Yeah, he was the CEO." He typed with his thumb on the number pad, and the phone buzzed again. "She says the official report is that he died in his sleep."

"Wow," Kara said. "I wonder what that means for the company."

"Probably not much," Michael said. "I'm sure they've got someone from the board ready to replace him or something. They always have contingencies for this sort of thing. Succession plans."

"He couldn't have been that old," Scott said.

Michael shook his head. "My age, maybe. Early sixties, I'd guess."

"Hey," Michelle said, nodding at the front doors. "There's R.J."

All heads turned toward the doors. R.J.'s hands were in the pockets of the grey and brown flannel hunting jacket he always wore, a couple days worth of scruffy beard on his face, which bore his characteristic wooden scowl. He saw the group standing by the bar and walked toward them.

"Hey, R.J.," Michelle said, raising her cash-filled hand in a small wave. And then the cash and receipts were in the air and Michelle's brain matter was splattered across the bar, across the pilsner glasses and the high-ball glasses and the margarita maker and the bottles of mid-range bourbon. And flecks of Betty's blood joined Michelle's brains half-a-second later, a grizzly mess of red and grey and black on the brown bar.

Many people seem to think that a gun when it goes off makes a sound like a cannon or a stick of dynamite, powerful and thunderous and deep, but this usually is not true, at least not with the types of guns most have the opportunity to fire. They are, however, quite loud, even when equipped with a silencer, which only makes the sound of gunfire softer and higher pitched, but hardly quieter.

Take a gun like this one, for example: A Tauron Model 748SS Pro Edition .380 ACP, with a compact, stainless steel frame, smooth trigger, and checkered grip, and which is only just over five inches long and finished with white stainless steel, except now it has very tiny dots of red on it. This gun, even with the homemade silencer fashioned from a small black Maglite, is loud enough that Joe, the fat chef who'd been in prison once, several years ago, for too many instances of driving while under the influence, but who hadn't in the time since then gotten behind the wheel of a car after more than four beers, heard the shots and ran out of the BOH through the door with the big YES on it and into the FOH and got shot in the neck, right through the jugular, by R.J. Frederickson, who saw him coming through the door.

There was only one woman left standing in the dining room

now, Kara, and to her credit she let out only a shriek, not a long, drawn-out, annoying sort of scream, and so R.J. didn't immediately shoot her but instead turned the gun toward his boss, Geoff McCree.

"Down!" R.J. ordered, waving the gun more than a little wildly. "On the floor. All of you!"

They obeyed his command, each of them, and R.J. noted that the fuckin' geriatric one dropped a cell phone which flew apart when it hit the floor and he was shaking visibly as he sunk to his knees into the slick pool of dark red that was pouring from Betty's lifeless body. R.J. willed the old man to not have a heart attack.

He'd had been planning this for weeks, not that there was much to plan. R.J. was a quick thinker, a real sharp guy, and he knew that when he came in he'd just make his move on the fly, shoot who he felt like shooting, drawing the whole thing out a bit before killing Geoff, and maybe raising the gun to his own damn head at the end of it all. He'd wanted to off a handful of customers, because they were all guilty of the same apathy and indifference, and he'd cursed silently when he walked into the foyer and noticed the dining room was empty. Not a fucking customer in the damn place. Not even the fucking hostess, who he'd wanted to shoot first, wanted to end her stupid teenage blondness. But then he'd seen everyone standing by the bar, grouped oh-so-conveniently together for him, and so he'd taken out two of the women, because why not. And now he'd slow things down for just a minute before getting on with it.

His friend, the black bear, stood behind him, dressed sanctimoniously in a baby blue terry cloth bathrobe, arms folded across his barrel-chested torso. "Well done, Richie," the bear said, whispering and shouting into R.J.'s left and right ears.

"Fuck off!" R.J. shouted, and the five hostages on the ground flinched.

"Not you," R.J. said to them, flicking the gun.

The bear had grown more and more real as the weeks went on, as they sat together at R.J.'s breakfast table and talked about how this day would play out.

"No, really, I mean it," the bear said in earnest. "I mean, look at that. Three shots. Three shots you fired and three people dead. That's really very good. Your marksmanship is remarkable . . . unless of course you're trying to kill me, but nobody's perfect, right?"

R.J. didn't turn toward the bear—turning was exactly what it would want him to do. It wanted to sabotage him. It wanted to sabotage it all. And yet this whole thing had been its idea. R.J. didn't know what it wanted.

R.J.'s jacket smelled of nicotine.

Scott—he was always so confident, R.J. thought—dared to speak. "Why are you—"

But R.J. shifted his aim and pulled the trigger, splintering the barstool behind Scott's head. "I said shut the fuck up!"

"Oh, so you're not going to actually shoot that one," the bear observed, his voice cool. "I see. You just want to prove how scary you are. Respect, right? But you'll still kill the boss man, yes? You've been saying you wanted to kill the boss man."

R.J.'s outstretched, gun-wielding hand began to wobble. His grip was too tight, and so he loosened it and relaxed and the wobbling stopped.

The black bear—he kept telling R.J. that he had a name, but that R.J. didn't deserve to know it—shuffled behind the bar and began making himself a cocktail. And of course R.J. was in the present moment consciously unaware of the impossibility of it all. "Would you like one?"

A phone rang, and R.J. recognized the ring: two short deep squawks and one high long one. He saw the phone on the floor next to Geoff's right knee, its screen cracked and green and lighting up. Geoff reached for it and R.J. moved forward, stepping on his hand. "Don't."

Geoff looked up at him. "R.J.," he said, "I don't know why you're doing this, I really don't, but my wife is having a baby right this second, and the number on that phone belongs to St. Elizabeth hospital. Please . . ."

R.J. saw expressions of surprise light across the faces of everyone else.

"Do you see that?" the bear said, sipping a sickly greenish brown concoction he'd garnished with a cherry and an olive and a lemon peel and a peppermint stick. "They didn't even know. He didn't even tell them. No wonder you hate this place so much. Did you know? I certainly didn't know." The black bear spat his drink out and set the glass on the bartop. "Actually, that's a lie—I knew. That drink is terrible, by the way."

The phone was still ringing. The Grill's voicemail was only on outside of business hours; during the day, it would ring and ring and ring either until the caller hung up or until someone answered it. The caller obviously wasn't hanging up.

"Come on, man," the bear said. "Let the guy pick it up. And then kill him."

R.J. took his foot off Geoff's hand. He placed the 748SS Pro Edition with the homemade silencer against Geoff's scalp at an angle an inch above his ear. It was likely he would tell whoever was on the other end what was going on, but it didn't matter. "Pick it up."

Geoff fumbled, and for a moment R.J. thought he might have broken the man's hand, but he managed to grip the phone and put it to his ear.

"Marla? Marla, calm down, what . . .? No. She's . . . she's okay? Let me talk to her. No, let me, let me . . . *let me talk to my wife, Marla!*"

R.J. flinched. Scott flinched. Michael flinched. Kara flinched. The bartender was calm and meditative. They'd never heard Geoff raise his voice, not once. Michelle and Betty and Joe didn't flinch, because they were dead.

"Elaine . . . dear. Is it a boy . . ."

Geoff McCree wasn't exactly crying, the phone against his ear, his hand throbbing, the warm metal of a recently fired gun against his head, but there was a sort of wetness on the high part of his cheeks, just below his eyes.

"It's a boy," his wife said. "He looks like you."

There was in his wife's voice no frustration, no trace of annoyance or anger.

"How are you doing?" Geoff asked.

"The surgery went fine," she said. "I've been in recovery the last hour, and they weren't going to let me call you, but I insisted."

She sounded tired.

"He's so beautiful, Geoff."

"I'm so sorry I wasn't there," Geoff said. "I'm so, so sorry."

"Hey," she whispered, "I know you wanted to. You have the restaurant, though. I understand."

The truth was, Geoff had felt more than terrible about his one-night affair with Cathy Blumstead, about the way he didn't care enough to even just not cheat on his wife. He thought about it all the time, wondered what was wrong with him. What part of him had died, and when and how long ago, that made him do these things, that made him not care and made him feel so little for so many. He was not a godly man, but if he was, if he cared enough to pray, he might have prayed now, silently, for some sort of forgiveness and redemption.

"No, no. Listen," he said, his voice low, its usual gruffness gone, "I'm not even at the restaurant now. I left. I quit, Elaine. Just a few minutes ago, I quit. I should have been there with you. I'm in the car now, though."

"You're . . . in the car."

"Yes, baby." Geoff felt the warm gun against his head. "I'm on my way to the hospital. I'll see you soon."

He heard his wife yawn on the other end. "I'll see you . . ."

"You get some rest. I love you."

"I love you too."

Geoff hung up the phone.

Selected Excerpts from the Unpublished Memoirs of Earl E. Bradford, Jr.

The truth is, I never set out to build a restaurant. The restaurant was Teddy's idea, and in the beginning, I was against it. I wasn't an entrepreneur like he was. He had his MBA. I'd just graduated with a Masters in agricultural science. I was going to buy a farm with the money I'd been saving my entire life. That's all I wanted: a farm and a wife, maybe a few kids.

I'd buy a bunch of land to start, and not in Texas but somewhere like Kansas or Idaho. I was leaning toward Kansas. I'd buy first just a little land, a few acres, and I'd buy a little trailer and plop it down in the middle of that land and that's where I'd live for the next few years, working hard everyday, up at the break of dawn, building the farm, planting fields at a first, corn or potatoes, lots and lots of fields because over time I'd buy more land, thousands of acres as the farm grew, and then I'd buy the animals, maybe first just chickens, and then cows, and some horses, pigs, a goat or two. The farm would be profitable. It would have barns and coops and pens and tractors and a silo, and only after all this was taken care of would I think about building a house, a big one with three or four bedrooms—enough for the kids—and a kitchen with only the best appliances, and an office and a den where we could watch television or read books together after a hard day's work, and a dining room large enough for a big table so that we could have guests—friends—over for supper and parties and conversation. I was twenty-three.

"You'll make it all back," Teddy said that day as we ate lunch at the diner across the street from the lot he was trying to convince me to buy. He told me that with my capital and his business knowledge, there wasn't a chance the idea could fail. He'd even put my name in the restaurant's name, he said, right there at the beginning of it. *Earl and Teddy's.* I wanted to ask him why, if he had these "business chops," he hadn't been able to come up with any capital of his own. But he was my older brother, he'd always been there for me. How could I say no?

So I'd push my plans back a year, is what I'd do, work on Teddy's restaurant first and *then* buy the farm.

Things just sort of snowballed.

* * *

I remember this one time, when I was ten and Teddy was fourteen, when our Pa took us to the state fair in Dallas. Ma was at home, recovering because she'd just miscarried for the third time.

We were eating caramel apples and walking around the back part of the fairgrounds, away from the rides and the games and the sideshow attractions, near the animals. We walked up to this horse, this prized stallion, wild and big and strong, muscles more like an ox's muscles than a horse's. It was just me and Teddy standing there with it—Pa was talking to the owner of this thousand-pound pig a few stalls away.

I remember I said something about how beautiful the horse was, something about it's mane, maybe, or about the white spots on its gray fur.

"You a fag?" Teddy said.

I didn't know what he meant.

"If you love the horse so much," he said, "why don't you marry it?"

I didn't understand what Teddy was getting at. I munched away at my caramel apple, which was a granny smith, so it was especially sweet, almost like candy covered in candy.

I don't know exactly what happened next, what Teddy did, but the horse started braying and hawing and freaking out, kicking the back of its stall with its hind legs. A half-dozen people rushed over to see what was going on, and Teddy grabbed me pulled me away and said, "Come on, this is boring. Let's go find Pa."

* * *

Teddy and I didn't see much of each other in the late '70s. He packed up and started traveling after we broke ground on our hundredth location, flying back only for the important business meetings and then taking off again. He seemed lost. I stayed in Austin and, for the most part, I ran things.

I worked in that first restaurant myself, cooking and managing, and I tried for a long time to do the same thing with each and every location we opened. Even when our growth rate became rapid, viral, I still made an effort to visit each store, work with the employees, show the cooks tricks I'd learned when working in the first one, make sure people new that the "Earl" in *Earl and Teddy's American Grill* was a real person, that I wasn't just a corporate man behind a curtain, that I'd put everything I had into this company and I hoped they would be dedicated enough to do the same.

* * *

I don't know how to write a memoir, but as we were revising my will last year, my lawyer suggested it was something I might want to do. I put it off for a long time, and even now as I write it, I'm not entirely sure what to do. I'm just transcribing bits and pieces of my life as they come to me.

Like the time Pa took me flying and let me try my hand at the controls. Ma was so mad when she found out I'd flown the little plane. I was way too young, she said, and what was my Pa thinking! But I loved it, my nine-year-old self floating high above the world, propellers on either side and in front of me, pulling this metal thing forward while I told it which way to go, to bank left or to turn slowly right, to pull up or to dip gently down, my Pa's strong hand on mine telling me "Gentle now. Don't pull too hard or you'll send us into a freefall, and trust me, we don't want that."

Or like the time, when Teddy and me realized we had a real thing on our hands here, something big and popular and that *we'd* created, and we decided that maybe we should open a second store.

Or like the time last year when I sat in the lawyer's office and wondered what happened to those two or three kids I wanted to have. Had someone else had them? Is that how that works? If a person isn't born somewhere, to someone and some particular situation, does their consciousness ever exist somewhere else? Are we predestined to exist as individual human beings? What if I'd been one those kids my Ma had miscarried—would I have ever existed then?

* * *

I remember the plane crash with vivid clarity, or at least I remember everything that happened after I woke up from the nap I'd been taking during the flight, exhausted from the managing of our ever-growing business, Teddy having been little help recently, busy preparing for the wedding. I woke to the sound of a loud crash, electricity on metal, followed by darkness and my Pa, an old man now with grey hair and wrinkled skin and a mind as sharp as ever, coming out of the cockpit and into the cabin and telling us that all the instruments had failed. He couldn't get control. "Remember what I told you about freefalls, son?" he said to me, winking.

My Ma looked scared. My Pa held her and told her he'd try the radio again, maybe it was working now, maybe he could call for help. I don't know if it was her fear or what, but Ma seemed to accept this as enough, to think that it would work and that we would be fine. Pa continued to hold her. He never did try that radio.

And Teddy. Well, to Teddy it seemed like nothing was happening at all. He held his head low and stared into the glass of champagne he was holding. Half of the glass's pink bubbly contents had spilled when the lightning struck and the plane jerked to the side. I could it see there, a dark spot on the front of silent Teddy's striped trousers.

I went back to sleep.

* * *

I really couldn't tell you how things happened the way they did between Elsa and I. I hadn't even met her until I woke up from the coma. Teddy hadn't introduced her to the family—he said he was saving that for the wedding. She was beautiful, though, standing there at the foot of my hospital bed, my attorney next to her, both of them ready to tell me what happened, that my family was dead but that the business was booming, that they were even in the process of putting together a private board of directors.

Few people know this, but Elsa and I separated last year, legally. She lives in Puerto Vallarta now, and though she has no stake in the company anymore, she still gets half my holdings.

* * *

The big question about the IPO was "Why?"

"Why now, Earl?"

"Not that we aren't pleased, Earl, but it just seems to us like this is coming out of nowhere."

"What exactly do you have up your sleeve?"

I'd been against an IPO for so long, but I don't suppose ever had much of a reason. I don't know. Maybe it was that I'd built this, this restaurant . . . empire, almost by myself, and I wanted it to stay that way. The Grill was my farm—that farm I'd never had the chance to buy and cultivate—casual fine dining the soil that I never got to till, steak and seafood and pasta dishes the crops I never got to grow, cooks and servers and middle managers the animals I never got to raise. I suppose that last one was a terrible analogy, but I was never a writer, so forgive me.

And I suppose this all sounds so morose, but that isn't my intention. I'm not disappointed in the way my life turned out. I may not have built a farm, but I still built *something*, something big and good. I don't sell crops, but people *eat at my restaurant*. And anyway, the agricultural industry is shot to hell now, in the twenty-first century.

*　*　*

I always found it peculiar, once I became old enough to understand just how peculiar a lot of things are, that Pa had named *me* Earl, after him, instead of Teddy, even though Teddy was born first.

*　*　*

I've got two houses now.

There's a penthouse in Manhattan, which I bought from some television star who was selling it so that she could move out to L.A. to do movies. That was decades ago that I bought it, and I've spent most of my summer months there ever since, because Austin in the summer is unbearably hot, and yes New York can still be hot but at least it's not so dry.

The second house is this one, here in Austin. It's big, but not so big that I don't see all of it most days. I designed it, but of course I paid others to build; I wouldn't have had time to do that myself. It's not a farmhouse, but that's okay. It's never been occupied by children, because I never had children, and that's not as okay, but it's what is. It has a pool, which I admittedly haven't used much since the arthritis started in my hip a couple years ago, but I use the hot tub all the time. I use the kitchen often, too, and the wet bar. I entertain at least once a week.

I am not unhappy, just a little tired, and I get this pain in my arm sometimes, and like I said, there's the arthritis, but I'm not unhappy. In fact, I've been blessed, is what I'd say to anyone who asked.

I don't think I ever heard about that television star appearing in a single movie.

THREE

Twelve Months Pre Brand-Changing Day, 2012

The rain fell hard on Scott as he waited on the sidewalk in Tarentum, Pennsylvania, twenty-two miles northeast of downtown Pittsburgh where his apartment near the Strip District had gone up in flames the day before. He'd told the authorities that he had a place to stay, and after being allowed into the blackened space in which he used to live, gathering the things that had survived the fire—some paperback books, a few DVDs, his black non-slip shoes, his laptop—because they were sitting on or near a shelf in the living room, which had (the living room) been scorched only in places and not completely charred like the rest of the apartment, he called Brooklyn Smalls, a former coworker from Groovy Burger with whom he'd slept a few times towards the end of his employment there, and she agreed that he could stay at her place for the night, but *only* for the one night, and then he had to be gone, out of there, she was done with him. And so he stayed with her that night and of course they slept together, but in the morning she kicked him out, furiously, and slammed the door behind him, and then it started to rain.

But Scott had called his mother the night before also. He was only in the heavy rain for an hour, his possessions in one of those small plastic storage boxes underneath his damp ass, when his mother's old rusted Honda Accord pulled up to the curb. The window rolled down and his mother popped her head out into the rain and called out, loudly over the falling rain, which was falling harder and harder with every second now, "Scott?"

Scott stood, jumped up really, unsure what to say or how to speak. He hadn't seen his mother in some time—a year, at least —despite living only an hour-and-a-half drive away, and he did feel bad about that, so he just picked up the plastic box with his things in it and hauled it around to the passenger side of the car and tried to open the back door, but the door was locked. He saw through the glass his mother make some sort of movement or gesture, and then there was a *click*—a sort of fast *click*, like a double *click*, like *click-click* but really fast—and he tried the door again, the plastic box with his things in the cradle of his right arm, and the door opened and he slid the box onto the back seat. The box wasn't heavy, but still, he was glad to be free of its weight.

He sat in the passenger seat in the front of the car, and as he buckled his seatbelt, his mother pulled away from the curb and back onto the road. Scott looked at his mother and then out the windshield and through the wipers and at the rain and then back at his mother. "I—" he said.

He was quiet and she was quiet.

"Thank you for picking me up," Scott said.

His mother took her eyes off the road for just a moment— she was a very careful driver—and looked at him. "Of course," she said. "You know I'm always here for you."

And then she said, "You look good."

And then she said, "What's with the beard?"

* * *

And so now they drove for just over two hours, stopping once at that newly constructed rest stop on 79 so Scott could pee and eat some breakfast—he bought an Egg McMuffin from the rest station's quaint little McDonald's, and of course he detested fast food and hadn't eaten it in something close to two years now, but he was hungry this morning and devoid of the energy to care about nutritional content or lack thereof or opposite thereof—neither of which he'd had a chance to do before being kicked out of Brooklyn Smalls' bed and apartment. Scott's mother was a slow driver. She was also young—thirty-seven now; when they went out for dinner together later that evening, Scott and his mother were mistaken for siblings—but she only looked young and *was* young; she didn't act young or feel young, but rather she exuded, almost wept, a sort of oldness. It was as if, Scott observed, all the people and all the things she'd known, all the actions she'd taken, all the harrowing big and little life events she'd activated and endured, all the tiny things and the massive things, all the minutiae, all the superfluous *ofs* and superfluous *thats*, had been absorbed into themselves, had formed this endless ball of energy that sat heavily on her heart chakra or wherever and that was released, one insignificant little measure at a time, with his mother's every leaden breath. But, Scott also knew, she'd never tell you this—you could only observe it and draw your own conclusions, and thus your conclusions, Scott's conclusions, could be very wrong, although Scott certainly didn't think they were.

Lydia Pelletier lived in a house in Austintown, just outside of Youngstown and in a nice area, on a nice street with dozens of similar houses: 2000 square-foot bi-levels with vinyl siding in either white or light blue or some variation of beige, occupied by husbands and wives who either were expecting a child, were raising children, or whose children had long been born and grown and moved on, the only exception on both counts being the older retired couple in the red house next door to his mother's house who both had smoker's coughs, which coughs were not as prominent as they once had been since quitting the habit five years ago, and whose forty-year-old son Bobby was divorced and broke and fat and living with them until he could get back on his feet again. It was the house Scott had grown up in, at least since he was six years old and his mother had reconciled with his grandmother and they'd moved here, to Ohio, and lived together, the three of them, quite happily. And then Scott's grandmother had died when he was eighteen, four years ago, her blood sugar climbing to dangerous and then deadly levels, which she had of course ignored until ketoacidosis set in, which she further ignored and then died. And so then Scott and his mother lived in that house, until Scott's search for growth and improvement shifted into arrogant egotism and he realized that he was too good for this town. After that, it was just his mother, and Scott hadn't even called her during his year away enough times that he could count them on more than one hand, the call after the fire included. It came as a surprise to him, then, when he returned to his childhood home and found his bedroom unchanged and that one painting he'd painted in high school still hanging on the cream-colored wall above the stairs next to a picture of a crucified Jesus.

"It still smells like home," Scott said after setting the plastic box with his things on the bed in his old room. Home was cinnamon and caramel and vanilla icing. Scott had a habit of denying home.

"That would be the candles," his mother said.

On the shelf above the television was a scented candle, unlit but in one of those electric warmers that kept the wax melted so that the scent of flowers or candy or artificial baked goods was constant but not dangerous in its being so. Scott hated the things —the scented candles—and the way they tickled his nose ad infinitum until his head hurt with artificiality, but he said nothing of his hatred now.

"Also the cinnamon rolls I baked this morning," his mother said, and from the kitchen she produced a tray of rolls, no longer warm but still fresh and gooey.

Scott was almost angry for a moment. She knew he didn't eat shit like this, but she always did this, made him crappy, shit-for-you food that she knew he didn't eat. But then again, he'd eaten McDonalds on the way here, so he took one of the cinnamon rolls and bit into it, and it was soft and delicious. "Thank you," he said. "They're very good. Thank you."

"I can put them back in the oven on low if you want," his mother said. "Warm them up a little for you. They're better that way."

Scott swallowed. "That's okay," he said. "Maybe later."

For all his perceived brilliance and cleverness, Scott hadn't foreseen the awkwardness that came with returning home. The shuffling and the silence. The initial lack of conversation. The him taking a shower and his mother doing housework. The him sitting in his childhood bedroom and paging through the paperbacks he'd left on the black wooden shelf there and his mother doing more housework. Like nothing had happened. Like Scott hadn't utterly failed at life again.

They went to dinner, Scott and his mother. They went to this Texas Roadhouse sort of deal a couple townships over. Scott ordered a ribeye, medium-rare, with a baked potato and grilled squash. He'd been a vegetarian for the last six months, Scott had, up until this morning when he'd ordered that sausage-egg-and-cheese from that rest station McDonald's. Scott's brief stint with vegetarianism hadn't been a product of trying to be healthier— he was already plenty healthy by that point, had lost his fifty pounds, and as far as he understood diet and nutrition, one could be very healthy eating meat as long as one also ate fruit and vegetables and avoided processed foods. That was the key to any diet, was Scott's opinion now: avoiding processed foods, which is why, when Scott became vegetarian and started hanging out with other vegetarians, he was able to feel smug and gloat in the smugness that came from being vegetarian and still eating healthy, from avoiding the processed foods while his other vegetarian friends ate faux-meats like soy burgers and "cheese" and Quorn. Scott was vegetarian because of, you know, the animals, because of love for living things. And sure Scott's vegetarian and vegan friends had cared about the animals, too, but Scott had really cared about these issues, couldn't they see, because Scott hadn't pretended to eat meat and cheese like everyone else. He had *sacrificed.*

He ordered a Shiraz with his pre-meal salad, and another Shiraz with his meal. His mother drank a Long Island and took generous forkfuls of her shrimp Alfredo.

"So now what?" Lydia asked, her hand wrapped around her beverage.

"What do you mean 'now what'?" Scott said.

"I mean, well, what now. I mean now that you're back here I mean. What are your plans?"

"I haven't thought about it much yet. I haven't exactly had a chance, y'know? I mean, yesterday I had a place to live and I had furniture and clothes and things, but now, I mean, well, now I don't, exactly." He didn't mention that, while, yes, he *had* had an apartment, chances he'd have made next month's rent were slim.

"And well what about that business you said you started? How's that going? Can you keep doing it here?"

"The business is dead."

"Oh."

"Yeah, it . . . it just didn't work out."

"I'm sorry to hear that. I know you were excited about it. You put a lot of work into it and everything, I know."

"Yeah, well. It just. I guess it just . . . I had a few jobs, a few clients, I mean, but the word never really spread. And all the big businesses in the city who I thought would maybe hire me already had people. They didn't want or need me. I'm really good, I know that, but the demand just isn't there."

"Yeah." His mother nodded, nibbled on her onion rings. The onion rings crunched as she bit into the thick breading. "And you've got savings, though?"

Scott nodded. "I've got savings. I mean, I have enough."

"Well, you know you're always welcome at home, Scott, as long as you need to or want to, you can stay with me."

"I know," Scott said. And then, sincerely: "I love you, Mom."

"I love you too, Scott. Always." She smiled.

Scott smiled back. His steak was cooked perfectly. Warm, red center. The Shiraz was good.

"What about a car?" His mother asked. "I know in Pittsburgh you didn't need a car, but you pretty much have to have a car around here, you know."

Scott didn't have enough money for a car, at least not one he'd feel comfortable driving. He'd sold his Prius when he'd moved to Pittsburgh. He had still owed on it and the sale had allowed him to pay it off. "I'll get a car. I just need to find one, I guess. Something used, right now, of course."

"I'll keep an eye out for you. See if I see anything about."

There was silence for a moment.

"And what about you?" Scott said, suddenly, impulsively, changing the subject. "How have you been? How's work and everything?"

Lydia smiled, and Scott recognized it as a genuine, happy smile. "It's actually going okay," she said. "I—. Well, there's sort of this someone that I'm seeing. Someone from work."

"*Mom.*" Scott grinned. "That's great."

His mother blushed. Scott couldn't remember the last time he'd seen her look embarrassed. Scott's mother had a good job now, a stable job, one that paid well and she enjoyed doing. When Scott and Lydia first moved to Ohio after reconnecting with Scott's grandmother, who had moved to Ohio herself four years prior, Lydia acquired a job as a secretary at a family doctor's office. A couple years later, the practice shut down (actually, the practice *was* shut down, in the passive sense, because the doctor, one Rich Fineman, M.D., was providing prescriptions for certain well-sought-after narcotics to patients who didn't need them in exchange for relatively copious sums of money), and Lydia was hired by a peculiar sort of dentist, a Chi Chi Chang, D.D.S., who smelled of rubber and Novocaine, and she kept that job for eight years before Dr. Chang flat-out retired, suddenly and without warning, and didn't even bother trying to sell his practice. Since then, Lydia had been working for Stephen Alan Fischer, an orthotist who, despite his pretension for using three names, was a good man and a good employer, and after not too long, he'd offered to send Lydia to Columbus to attend a week-long fitting class, and she'd come back a licensed fitter, which is to say whenever Dr. Fischer wasn't in the office, and sometimes when he was but was busy, it was her job to fit the various leg braces and foot orthotics on the patients, and her salary was substantially higher because of this.

Scott said: "*Well . . .*"

" 'Well' what?"

"Well what's his name?"

"Oh, I don't—"

"Come on, Mom. You're just going to dangle that little piece of information in front of me and then let it hang there?"

"Chris." His mother spurted the name.

"Chris. Chris is his name?"

"Yeah, well, it's—"

"That's fantastic. And so when do I get to meet Chris?"

"Oh, well, you know. It's not. I mean. I mean we're just sort of starting out, you know. It's only been a few weeks maybe."

She was grinning from ear to ear, trying to restrain the grin, to pull it back into a neutral expression, but her lips were like elastic, springing back up toward her eyes every time she tried to relax them. Scott knew the feeling, but he hadn't felt it since he was maybe like fifteen, since Cindy Carbuncle had agreed to go to homecoming with him freshman year.

"You're really happy, then, aren't you, Mom," Scott said, his voice's tone listing to that empty spot in the soul where breakthroughs and self-realizations are born.

"Yeah. Yes, I am." Her voice listed toward her eyes, with her smile.

And Scott knew then that he'd been wrong in his judgment of his mother: She wasn't sad or tired or heavy-hearted or any of that other petty self-pitying bullshit—that was him, not her. His mother was smiling and warm and peaceful.

"We are . . ." she said. "We're constantly told we can't be happy. All of us, I mean, but I mean women too, especially. Especially women. We watch these Lifetime movies, like two new ones every day, and if we had it their way we'd all be in abusive relationships or married to secret serial killers or freaking out because we've got cancer or because our child is sexting or being cyber-bullied. But that's not the truth, I've learned, Scott. They convince us that nowhere is safe, no home is truly a home, no place or person is a home. But I've learned, recently more so than ever, but I think it's something we're always meant to learn if we choose to. To learn it, that is. To be open to learning. That when you choose love, everywhere feels like home."

Scott nodded. She *was* happy.

And when Scott looked around, he saw dozens of people sitting in the dimly lit steakhouse. Some people were fat, some were thin, some were just beginning to grow a spare tire around the midsection; some people were old, some were young, some were somewhere in between; some people were with families or groups of friends, some were alone, and some were on first dates or second dates or third dates. And Scott felt pity for all of them. They were missing out, he told himself—they weren't growing; they didn't even probably know what real growth meant, what "personal growth" meant, not like Scott did. These poor people with their lives and their steakhouse meals. This is what Scott always thought when he looked at most other people, at "normal people," "the masses." But now Scott also wondered if maybe he was wrong in judging them so.

* * *

Scott found an apartment two weeks later. He appreciated his mother's willingness to accept him once again, but he needed to be on his own (he couldn't very well take dates back to his mother's house, could he?). He had enough money for a couple months' rent for a small place downtown—the same money that was barely enough for Pittsburgh was enough to last him a small while in Youngstown—and once he moved there, he set about reclaiming the freedom he always felt so close to attaining. He didn't get a job—he couldn't get a job, not like a normal person, not again, and he'd notice when he made judgments like this, sometimes he'd notice, and he'd try to be conscious of them like he'd learned to be conscious of everything because he was so committed to growth. And so all day he read and worked out and sat at his computer, which was getting old and sluggish and the poly-carbonate of which was cracking in the corner near the screen, searching Craigslist for creative gigs, some of which he found and contacted the poster about and accepted and made a little money from, enough money for food anyway. He didn't buy a car. He still had faith that, if he *thought positively* and *committed to growth*, then one day soon the opportunities would just come pouring in, just you wait and see. And he took the bus once or twice to visit his mother in Austintown, but other than that, even though he was only ten miles away, he rarely saw her.

"Hello?"

"Hello, yes. Yes, hello."

"Um, hello."

"Yes, I'm sorry. Hello. Um, is this . . . is this Scott Palleteer."

"It's pronounced Pelletier, like with an a on the end. It's French. But yes, this is he."

"Yes, um, hello, Scott. Mr. Pelletier."

" . . . "

"This is . . . my name is Officer Ben Moransky with the Austintown Police Department."

"Okay."

"Um, we tried reaching you at your home but couldn't find an address—"

"Have I done something wrong? What is this—"

"Oh. No no. No, you've done nothing wrong. Listen."

" . . . "

"Listen, I'm very sorry to have to tell you this. Oh, wait, wait. You are . . . you are related to Lydia Pelletier, yes?"

"Yes. I'm her son."

"Yes, I see. Well, um. I'm very sorry to tell you this, Mr. Pelletier, but your mother was found dead this morning in her home."

" . . . "

"It, uh, it appears to have been suicide."

"I see."

"I'm so sorry, Mr. Pelletier. I'm so very sorry."

" . . . "

"Do you, um, do you have any questions? If you'd like, we can—"

"No, no that's okay. Thank you, Officer."

It was shock is what it was. Scott sat on his couch, which was used and blue and lonely, for several hours. He thought about drinking a beer, but he had no beer, so he just sat. He picked up his copy of *How to Win Friends and Influence People*, opened it to a random page and started reading, but the words meant nothing, and he threw the book across the small room and into the wall. He fell asleep like that, sitting on the couch, staring forward and to the left just a little, at the open book on the floor. When he awoke late the next morning, the shock was mostly gone, and he picked up his phone and redialed the last number that had called.

Scott's mother had been found in bed, alone, by a female coworker who had come by to pick her up for a scheduled breakfast. The house had been clean, tidy, unmolested. The medics and police would likely have assumed natural causes, if not for the empty bottle of Mosquito Away Insect Repellent lying open on the kitchen counter next to the sink.

N,N-Diethyl-meta-toluamide (DEET), the main ingredient of most insect repellents, had this way of inhibiting a certain enzyme—acetylcholinesterase—in the central nervous system, and acetylcholinesterase played a role in the hydrolysis of acetylcholine, a neurotransmitter. So what had happened was, most likely, Scott's mother had ingested, obviously on purpose, the entire bottle of Mosquito Away, and too much acetylcholine had accumulated at the synaptic cleft, leading to neuromuscular paralysis, which meant that Scott's mother then couldn't breathe. So it was asphyxiation—the cause of death. And Scott wondered why the doctors or the police couldn't just tell him that. Why did they need days for a damned autopsy when he'd been able to figure the whole thing out with a fucking five-minute wiki search?

Further investigation into Scott's mother's personal life revealed substantial debts, including hundreds of thousands of dollars worth of gambling debt incurred in casinos in Las Vegas, Atlantic City, and Los Angeles. Scott, when he heard this, failed to understand how it could be possible—his mother wasn't a gambler; she'd been, Scott always thought, irrationally frugal; and as far as he knew, she hadn't traveled outside Ohio once since they'd moved here sixteen years ago. But then things grew clearer: the police found odd patterns in Lydia Pelletier's financial records that strongly pointed to evidence of identity theft: Lydia might have spent three hours on a phone sex line from a number in San Francisco while her employer confirmed that she was, in fact, at work that day; or her social security number might have been used to collect a tax return in Kingman, Arizona, throwing a blip on the system that no one had bothered to investigate; or Lydia may have registered to vote in L.A. while also being registered in Mahoning County, Ohio (this was one of the most peculiar incidents, the police said, because what sort of criminal is so inclined that he cares about voting anyway?). But, Scott and the police wondered, if Lydia Pelletier were aware of these inconsistencies, why had she not simply reported them? This question was only answered when they found the letters and emails threatening not just Scott's mother's life, but Scott's life as well, if Lydia so much as said a word to anyone about the financial problems she was having. The emails even had attached pictures of Scott's mother in her home, clearly taken from her own computer's webcam. The police launched a full-scale investigation. They arrested Raul Vega Gonzales, Scott's father, only three days later; the man was in a Reno motel room with a prostitute, and they were both so coked up that they could do nothing but sit and stare as Reno police broke through the door and ordered them to get on the ground, now! And despite all this, the bank still took Scott's mother's house, car, and other possessions as compensation for the debt.

*   *   *

It was raining during Scott's mother's funeral. It always rains during fictional funerals—no matter what book or movie, comedy or tragedy, it always rains and the sky is always grey, and everyone holds black umbrellas. The turnout was larger than he'd expected, more than a hundred people, but Scott knew only a couple dozen of them. He said nothing during the service, just sat and listened, but afterward he shook hands and accepted hugs and said thank you, thank you, yes, it means a lot that you came, thank you.

"Scott."

Scott didn't recognize the woman. She had long dark hair and sad eyes and was probably in her early forties. Another coworker, most likely. "Thank you for coming," Scott said. "It means a lot that you're here."

"Oh, Scott," the woman said, and there were tears in her eyes, and she hugged Scott, her embrace tight and suffocating. "I've heard so much about you. I'm so sorry."

"Thank . . . thank you," Scott said. The woman broke the embrace, and when she leaned back and looked him in the eyes, Scott saw something familiar in the face of this woman he'd never met before. "I'm sorry, what was your name?"

"I'm . . ." the woman hesitated. "My name is Christine. I . . . worked with your mother. I was the one who found her, that morning."

Scott's eyes were suddenly wet. His cheeks were suddenly wet. Christine's shirt was wet as she hugged him once again. The next days melted together in Scott's imperfect memory, and even twelve months later it was only some sort of nebulous blur of dinner with Christine; of discussing his mother and how neither of them knew of the problems she was having, and Scott reflected openly on how we never really know, do we?, what another person might be up to in their heart, because here for years Scott had assumed his mother oblivious, had consciously withheld the details of his own life from her and most everyone else because, well, because they would never understand, and he thought himself so wise and growing that he might be the only one who did such a thing, and but here the entire time his mother had done the same, and Scott wondered now if everybody maybe, even just a little bit, held back, and maybe that was the problem, or maybe he'd been right all along, because here also he was only a few weeks ago thinking that maybe he'd been wrong to judge, because he assumed his mother was unhappy, and then she showed him just how happy she was, and he thought he saw that happiness in her eyes and in her uncontrollable smile and he thought *Oh, wow, I was so totally wrong*, and but then she'd killed herself, and then . . .; of laughing with Christine when they discussed his mother's more eccentric habits, those quirks and foibles like drinking white wine out of a collins glass, like hating to sit down and watch a movie unless the movie was *When Harry Met Sally*, which she watched often, like keeping an herb garden on the back porch, like baking literally *all the time*, like tugging on her earlobe to try and recreate the popping noise it had made one time when she'd done it years ago; of Scott asking "What the hell am I supposed to do now, because I thought I had it figured out"; of Christine saying "I don't know"; of Christine telling Scott that she really loved his mother; of Christine going to live with her brother in Delaware for a while because she needed a change of scenery; of Scott saying "I know that feeling" and telling her he was really glad to have met her and to have had the opportunity to get to know her over the last few days; of Scott walking into The Grill, two months after having returned to Youngstown, rent due in a week and dreading that he'd need to ask his landlord for an extension already, down to his last fifty dollars, and asking for an application.

"And so, then, Scott, tell me a little about yourself."

Some Time Pre Brand-Changing Day, 2012

"'Taco Bell: We make tacos! Kinda.'"

"That's a good one, Scott. Oh, I know, how about this one: 'Wendy's: Do what tastes right, which we swear isn't supposed to have any sort of sexual connotation, even though it does sound rather dirty, if not grammatically incorrect.'"

"I like that. Or: 'IHOP: Come hungry, leave obese.'"

"No, more like: 'IHOP: Come hungry, leave disgustingly overstuffed for like an hour and then suddenly get really hungry again because all you ate was a buttload of empty carbohydrates.'"

"'Pizza Hut: Gather 'round the crappy stuff.'"

"'Papa John's: Better ingredients than Pizza Hut, better pizza than Pizza Hut, still not that great, though.'"

"'Olive Garden: When you're here, you're family. Specifically, you're Big Jim's family. Big Jim killed his parents with a shovel when he was nine years old, but it's okay because he was only tried as a minor and got out of prison a few years ago and his probation officer said it was okay if he worked here, so he's our dishwasher now. Also, his brother went missing last week, but Big Jim swears he doesn't know anything about that.'"

"'Applebee's: Eatin' good in the neighborhood, which has

recently been plagued with outbursts of violent crime, specifically armed robbery. Seriously, like three houses on this street have been robbed in just the last two weeks, and someone was even shot at the last one, but don't worry because it was just a minor flesh wound and he'll be out of the hospital in a day or two and we've set up a neighborhood watch program so things should get better. Just tell your watch leader if you see anything suspicious.'"

"'Goodbye, Ruby Tuesday.'"

"'The Grill: Where everybody who hates food, their money, or themselves, eats.'"

"'Hooters: Delightfully tacky, yet unrefined.'"

"Dude, Mike, that's Hooters' actual slogan."

"Well, I mean, yeah, but it fits, doesn't it? You've got to admit that it fits."

"Very true. Hooters ain't bad, though."

"It's not?"

"No, no it's not, not really. Well, I mean, yes they are, but they're no worse than any of the other chains out there, and at least they're honest about it. You've got to respect Hooters for their lack of pretense. I've got a lot of respect for Hooters. Like this place, this place, The Grill, we constantly play ourselves up as this fancy, but not really actually fancy—because we don't want people to not eat here because they think we think they're beneath us—place, when in reality we actually totally suck, right. Like, our food isn't all that special, and our atmosphere, especially now with all the changes coming, just has this air of fakeness about it, and yeah, Hooters' food kind of sucks, too—well except for maybe their wings, *maybe*—but they don't pretend that it doesn't. They're all about exploiting women with big breasts, and they know and admit it, and that's cool with them and it's cool with the people who eat there. And I have a great deal of respect for all that, you know?"

"Yeah. I suppose you do have to respect Hooters."

The End of Brand-Changing Day, 2012

When Brand-Changing Day was over—when the police had come and asked their questions, when the bodies had been taken away, when a team with strong disinfecting chemicals, wearing goggles and blue gloves and yellow Hazmat suits, had set about cleaning up the mess they'd left behind—four people were dead, two shot in the forehead, one in the jugular, and one cleanly through the temple, and R.J. Frederickson was in custody, refusing to speak or look anything but unremorseful.

Scott sat at the bar in O'Darren's Pub, waiting for his drink. He'd ordered a whiskey and soda and he hadn't really specified which kind, so he hoped he would get a good whiskey, something premium and good and not any of that well shit, and he hoped Tommy behind the bar knew that by soda he'd meant soda water, and not like Coke or Pepsi or Diet Coke or Sprite or anything like that, just plain, simple, burns-your-throat-in-that-pleasantly-painful-way soda water. Club soda. The television was just above the bar. It was one of those 21-inch plasma or LCD deals, but Tommy behind the bar didn't have the resolution or the input or the brightness or something set quite right, and so the picture wasn't as clear as it should have been. The picture was blurry and hurt Scott's eyes, but he watched it anyway.

On the television, the 11 PM news was in progress,

anchored by Garry Brady because Mark Gonn is off tonight so I'll be filling in. We start tonight with the tragic story of a quadruple murder, a massacre—

There was a whiskey and club soda on the bar in front of Scott. He never saw Tommy set it down, but there it was. Scott picked up the glass. It was cold and solid in his hand, and bits of condensation covered the glass and moistened Scott's hand. There was very little light in O'Darren's at this time of night, but Scott found some and held the glass up to it. The mixture was light brown, golden almost. Through it Scott could see the television, the blurry picture diffused through the glass and the spirits and the ice, and the picture was incomprehensible except for shapes and colors, blobs of blue and green and red, except that they were all bronze now, colored by the spirits. Everything, all of it, is colored by our spirits. Scott hadn't even had a drink yet, and here he was already thinking drunk thoughts and missing details and staring out into space, and he knew that it was just the fear grasping hold of him, the fear and the joy and the uncertainty. He knew it was just because he was leaving and never coming back again. He was shaking. Nobody else could see it, but he was shaking. Inside he was shaking. Outside he was shaking. The ice clattered against the inside of the glass. It chinked against the edges like tiny little bells. Blue and green and red. Blobs on the other side of the liquid. Scott put the glass on the bar. He stared at it, but he wasn't thirsty. It was probably well whiskey anyway.

A man sat down next to Scott at the bar. He bumped his elbow into Scott's elbow and apologized. It's alright, my friend. The man ordered a Bud Light. They were only a dollar in bottles tonight. Scott looked at the man, but he wasn't really a man at all. He was wearing a letterman jacket and baseball cap with the bill on backwards and had the beginnings of a goatee poking out from the bottom of his chin, but it wasn't really working out for him. He took his Bud Light and walked away from the bar.

Scott smiled. The more he thought about it, the more he smiled. What happened next didn't really matter, he was realizing. It would matter when it happened, but right now there was just the music and the night. He looked around. He wasn't the only one there tonight. They were all there. Somewhere. Kara was there because her daughter was with her, the daughter's, father. Mike was there. There he was sitting in a booth with Kara and Angie. Angie was there. Scott hoped she was doing well. He knew she was doing well because she always seemed to be doing well, no matter how poorly she was doing. Maybe he would join them in a minute. He would. He'd join them at the booth in a minute.

And there was the other Mike, Michael, the manager-no-longer-in-training, sitting at the other end of the bar. He was wearing a plaid shirt and a dark grey polar fleece vest. His grey hair Scott had never realized was so long. He saw Scott and Scott nodded to him, and Michael nodded and tipped his beer toward the sky. Michael had been in Vietnam. He'd taken R.J. down.

"Is everything alright?" Tommy behind the bar asked.

Scott told him it was just fine, and he thanked him for the whiskey and cradled the glass in his hand like he planned on drinking it any second now. The beads of condensation moistened his hands again.

Scott stood up from the barstool, stepped away from the bar, the whiskey in his hand. He turned toward his friends' booth, and it looked so far away across the pub. There was an empty spot next to Mike, and probably Josh would be joining them later, and if he did, he could pull up a chair at the end of the booth. Scott headed over to join his friends for one last night.

But he didn't make it, because there was Lori standing right in front of him. "Hey," she said.

"Hey," Scott said.

They stood there for a bit, just stood there. Mike and Kara and Angie could see them from their booth. They all held their drinks and their breath, and they weren't chatting anymore, but were watching Scott and Lori across the pub.

And Scott said, "How'd you get in?"

Lori said, "I snuck in the back. Through the kitchen."

"Oh."

Lori said nothing.

"You missed a crazy day."

"Yeah, I had class."

"Yeah, I know." Scott still held the ice-cold glass. His hand was going numb. "I'm glad you're here."

"I'm glad you're safe."

Scott started to say something, but hesitated. There was a sort of pressure in his chest. He set the whiskey down on the nearest table, never mind the people sitting there. He turned to Lori, put his cold hands on her shoulders. He looked at her big icy blue eyes with their hint of eyeshadow and her pale skin with its hint of blush and her long curly flaxen hair. "Listen," he said. "I'm . . . I'm leaving tomorrow."

She nodded. "Yeah, I know," she said. "Kara sent me a text."

"That's why I'm glad you're here. I want you to know that I'm going to miss you. I wasn't going to tell you I was leaving, but after . . . now I'm glad you're here."

"I want to come with you. Wherever you're going."

Once upon a time, O'Darren's Family Pub was called O'Darren's Bar and Grill.

Some Time Post Brand-Changing Day, 2012

There's this calm in the air today for Eddie Juan Orenzo. There's this calm and this peace and this delightful sense of every-thing-just-is-and-that's-okay. Eddie can feel the sun beating down on his back as he walks up to the front doors, can feel the sweat on the nape of his neck, and so he takes his hat—it's a baseball cap, black and plain—off and uses it to wipe off his forehead and then his neck and then he tucks it into the back pocket of his tattered light-blue jeans.

He reaches out for the door on the left, pulls it open, and it's heavy but not too heavy, and he steps into the building, into the foyer, and is hit—affronted—with a burst of cool air that almost literally freezes the sweat that he used his baseball cap to smear across his forehead and his neck's nape. The air is on, obviously, and it's not always on, so he should probably be grateful even though he knows it will make little difference once he gets back into the kitchen, because back there the air is always broken these days and no one ever fixes it, and even if they did the heat from the grills and the fryers and the hot water would be too much, and so anyway.

There's a girl standing there at the hostess stand, and he recognizes her—that is, he's seen her before—but he doesn't know her name so he calls her Mammita. "Hello, Mammita," he says. He doesn't know any of their names—the other employees, but especially the girls, the waitresses and hostesses and even that one girl they've got working in the kitchen now—so he calls them all Mammita, the girls anyway, and he sees that it makes them giggle and whisper amongst themselves about Eddie the Dishwasher.

He's not interested in them—the girls—and it's not that he doesn't like women, because he does, but he's married. His wife's name is Maria and she's beautiful and has long almost jet-black hair except for those few strands of grey that have appeared in the last year and that he likes so she doesn't color them or anything like that, and her skin is tanned, and her eyes are very blue. She's pregnant, and Eddie is happy because the doctor says it's going to be a boy, and it'll be their first boy, their third child but their first boy, and that's exciting, and they'll probably name him Miguel after Eddie's father. His oldest daughter's name is Elsa, and she's sixteen—sixteen and he can hardly believe time's moved so fast—and she's smart and really likes fashion, and she just saved up all of her money so she could buy a new computer and scanner and a whole slew of sketchbooks and expensive but high-quality colored pencils. His other daughter is seven now; her name is Veronica, and her birthday was just last Wednesday. They'd had a party with all of her friends and some relatives and there was this big chocolate cake with a sort of cherry sauce filling right near the top, right near the icing but still separated from the icing by another smaller layer of cake, and Veronica wants to be a pony when she grows up or a doctor or a ninja, and Eddie tells her that doctor would probably be easiest, and she says maybe she doesn't want to be a doctor then, if it's so easy, and Eddie says that it's not *easy*, just easier than being a pony or a ninja. Eddie's mother lives with them, too—his Mama.

She's seventy-eight and one might think that she'll probably die soon, but she's still smart, whip-snap smart or however it goes, and she's full of energy and has the garden in the back yard that she tends, so they—Eddie and his wife and his Mama and his two daughters and soon his son—always have fresh tomatoes and peppers and lettuce and onions and garlic and this year his Mama is even growing strawberries, and his Mama raised him and his brother, who's in jail now, by herself with no help from nobody, and he loves her and respects her and will take care of her 'til the day she dies.

The girl—Mammita—looks up from her computer at the hostess station where she's standing and typing something and smiles. "Hi, Eddie," she says. And Eddie kind of smiles a little but more just nods his head and walks by.

Eddie is forty-five, and he lives over on the west side in what's not a terrible neighborhood but isn't the best neighborhood either, but it's just drugs and boozers that's the problem—nobody's ever died or been shot or anything like that, and everybody gets along and are good neighbors to each other —but sometimes Eddie does worry about the drugs, especially the hard ones like heroin and stuff, because he used to do them himself way long ago, way back when he was in his teens and twenties, and Elsa is in her teens now so he worries about her and the drugs, but he doesn't think she's touched them yet and he hopes she never will. Eddie's lived over on the west side his entire life, but not in the same house, not even on the same street but still. He's okay there, but he doesn't want his kids to stay there forever like him.

He was right—the air *is* still broken in the kitchen, and he can tell as soon as he opens the big door that says YES and walks through. But ah well, because he has his hat and will just keep wiping his forehead when it gets sweaty. He sees the new manager, Michael, and Michael is the only person whose name Eddie really knows, because well he's the manager, and Eddie likes him enough and but still he thinks it's a shame, what happened to Geoff and everybody. But Michael is good. Michael sees him and says, "Hey, Eddie."

Eddie walks up to one of the pop machines. He grabs a big styrofoam cup, which are new and are actually smaller than the old big Styrofoam cups, and which they're allowed to use now, and he scoops up a little bit of ice with the cup and holds it under the Coke spout and uses the cup to press the lever. And the Coke makes a *spfffffffft* sound as it hits the ice and fills the cup and foams over the edge. Eddie waits a few seconds for the foam to die down and then presses the cup against the lever again.

Eddie started working at The Grill when he was twenty-five. That was twenty years ago and the restaurant had just opened, which means he's worked here far longer than anybody else who works here now or ever did work here. Because he's been here so long, Eddie makes fifteen dollars an hour, and he works six days a week for six or seven hours in the evening from five o'clock to eleven or twelve. It doesn't cost much to live on the west side, so Eddie does alright even though he takes care of a lot of people, and they haven't told their daughter yet, but he and Maria have enough money put away to take care of Elsa when she goes to college, and by the time Veronica goes to college, they'll have enough for her too.

The foam at the top of the cup fizzles and dies out again, and the cup is full enough now, so Eddie grabs a lid and a straw and pops the lid onto the cup. As he turns around, trying to shove the straw through the little hole in the lid but for some reason the lid and the straw don't seem to want to cooperate, he nearly bumps into a young man who must have been standing right behind him waiting to use the pop machine.

"Sorry," the young man says a little softly.

"'S okay, *hermano*," Eddie says. The young man is maybe twenty. He has that sort of shaggy hair that's popular, and he probably can't grow a beard. Eddie has never seen him before. "You new?" he says.

The young man kind of nods. "Yeah."

"'S your name?"

The kid's eyes try to find something to look at other than Eddie's eyes. "Keith," the kid says.

"Keith," Eddie says, and he thinks that he might remember the kid's name for some reason. "Server."

"Yeah."

"I'm just the dish guy."

The kid, the young man, shuffles his feet and his shoulders sway from side to side, and Eddie realizes the kid is afraid or uncomfortable. But still he says, "What, you don't like dish guys or somethin'?"

The kid looks down. "I don't have anything against dish guys."

Eddie actually kind of laughs. "Course you don't," he says, "Nobody does because they're, we're, over the corner in a little hole by ourselves."

The kid is quiet, and Eddie kind of laughs again, but he's just having fun and thinks the kid might actually be a little scared, so he finally gets the straw through the lid and walks over to the dish station. He hears one of the Mammitas say to the kid something like, "That's just Eddie," or something.

Eddie likes beer like Corona with lemon but not lime and

Miller 64 and even Budweiser is okay as long as it's not Bud Light. He likes burgers and pork chops and tacos like his wife makes them—with corn tortillas and lots of chili powder and a mixture of pork and beef—and enchiladas like his Mama makes them—with her homemade enchilada sauce and chicken and fresh chilies and tomatoes from her garden. He likes to do push-ups and has the biceps and chest to prove it, although he's let the rest go a bit. He keeps his head shaved in the summertime but lets his hair grow in the winter. His wife likes it better shaved. He likes *CSI Miami* and wouldn't mind living in Miami but isn't angry or sad that he doesn't. He likes to read, but not every day or anything. He's been reading that new book by John Grisham for the last few weeks. He owns one suit, but he hasn't worn it since his brother was in court. He usually wears baggy worn-out jeans and larger-than-necessary t-shirts, but only because he likes them and they're comfortable. He likes his house. He loves his wife. He loves his Mama and his daughters so much.

There are dirty dishes—big round entree plates, soup bowls, soup cups, salad plates and side plates, the large round shallow bowls that they serve pasta in—piled all the way up to the glass racks, which are full, so high that they can't physically be stacked any higher because there's a big slanted metal shelf in the way. Eddie makes sure the dish machine is on and that there's detergent in the detergent thing, and he picks up a green dish rack and sets it on the counter above the food trap, and he takes a large entree plate and sprays it with the high-pressure hose and sets it gently in the dish rack. And then he takes another plate and does the same, except this one has a particularly stubborn something stuck to it, so he uses a piece of steel wool to scrape it. And then he sprays and racks another plate in front of that one. And keeps doing that, keeps taking the plates and the bowls and the other dishes and spraying them and scraping them and racking them, running the racks through the machine one by one. The stacks of dishes get smaller until they almost disappear, until there's almost nothing on the counter, and then the servers and the cooks bring more dirty things over, dishes and utensils and pots and baking pans, and Eddie sprays and scrapes and racks and washes.

ACKNOWLEDGEMENTS

Over the last year, I've learned that it takes a whole team of people to make a great book. The invaluable team who made *Brand-Changing Day* possible, and who I'd like to henceforth thank profusely, includes, but is not limited to (which is just another way of saying I'm sorry if I forget anybody here): Joshua Fields Millburn, without whose valuable input this book's ending would have been quite different; Ryan Nicodemus; Colin Wright, the best cover designer ever; Tahlia Meredith, who was willing to read the book in its entirety pretty much every time I made the smallest change; Samuel Engelen; Emily Tripp; Kathy Tu; R. Silver; Mike Pettacio, who I bounced the novel's original concept off of until he suffered bruises; Devon Boen; my family; the wonderful group of interns working for Asymmetrical Press; the amazing crew with whom I worked at a certain American chain restaurant; and like a hundred other people. I owe you all way more than hugs.

ABOUT THE AUTHOR

Shawn was born in San Diego, California, in 1990, where he lived until he was seven.

In high school, he won several awards both as a writer for and editor-in-chief of his student newspaper, prompting him to study journalism before deciding that his passion for writing was better directed at fiction.

Shawn currently lives in Helena, MT, with his fiancé.

OTHER WORKS BY SHAWN MIHALIK

The Flute Player

Brand-Changing Day: A Novel

Particles: A Novel

ENDNOTES

1. Many of the following instances are easily interchangeable; i.e. examples of your poor business sense may also work under examples of why you lack compassion.

2. Which paunch, by the way, has grown, if not significantly, at least noticeably since I began my employment with you. This isn't healthy. As you may have heard, there is an obesity epidemic in our country, and it turns out it is primarily caused by lack of exercise coupled with an inflated (pun totally intended; like, seriously, I spent a significant amount of time trying to choose between "inflated," "engorged" or "expanded") consumption of sugar, grains and other highly processed foods. I imagine it's no coincidence that I've never seen you do a push-up or that you rarely (never?) make a trip to the Create Your Own Garden Bar (*sic.* Customers are neither creating their own Garden Bar, nor is said bar a bar at which they create their own garden), and I'm sure the stress of working in a high-pressure restaurant job does your health no favors. Trust that I make these comments from a place of genuine concern.

3. Note that, if you did cut said employees, you would then lower your payroll expenses (i.e. it would cost you less).

4. It's okay to refuse to grant a customer a reservation when granting them a reservation wouldn't make any discernible sense. Remember: saying no is

actually saying yes to other things, which in this case can be interpreted as: saying "no, we can't take your party of fifteen right now," is the same as saying "yes, we would love to give our other customers exceptional service."

5. This is, of course, slight hyperbole on my part; viz. I'm exaggerating.

6. Bissell, by the way, is a very specific brand of vacuum, a brand to which our sweepers do not belong. Ours are Fuller Brand.

7. I don't know about anybody else, but I remedy this by simply ignoring it: if I choose a sweeper that doesn't work and thus fail to clean my floors sufficiently, it's hardly my fault, since because the broken sweeper is in the supply room, it is clearly manager-approved.

8. But here are a few: The manner in which you handled Angie's termination. The fact that you drove poor Katie to quit by consistently treating her with a lack of respect. The instance just this last week during which I, who was first-cut, was given a party of eleven at 8:00 PM, and therefore I, who, again, was first-cut, didn't leave the building until 11:00 PM. (I realize that this wasn't your decision—rather, it was R.J.'s—but *nemo mortalium omnibus horis sapit*.)

9. And here there is irony, because Trappist beers typically *would* be served in glasses less than 16 oz., but we don't serve Trappist beers, only things like Sam Adams and Blue Moon and Miller Light.

10. And with it let's delete such phrases as "casual fine dining" and "simple fresh American dining," which are oxymorons and mouthfuls respectively.

11. The infamous spicy cheese fondue, for example has 1224 , and a single garlic cheese biscuit has 110 (which granted may not be much of a problem since we only serve like one per person).

12. And even then I have to be sure to request the non-use of that garlic/margarine concoction, and who knows what's in the marinade.

13. And also because Joe cooks steaks perfectly.

14. Meatloaf, specifically meatloaf covered in a mysterious "meatloaf sauce," no matter what you tell yourself, along with deep-fried mozzarella sticks, southwestern-style spring rolls (which by definition are not spring rolls), and cajun jambalaya pasta (which by definition is not jambalaya), hardly constitutes "real food."

15. But if you wish to fire me outright, I understand, because well now things are just a bit awkward aren't they?